MW01488452

HEALING
HERITAGE

THE LOVE LEGACY
Book Four

A.F. VOYLES

aBM

Published by:
A Book's Mind
PO Box 272847
Fort Collins, CO 80527
www.abooksmind.com

Copyright © 2018
ISBN: 978-1-949563-01-6
Printed in the United States of America

Dedication

This book is dedicated to my husband for his patient and enduring love. Thank you, honey, for loving me like Jesus loves His bride– sacrificially, unconditionally and steadfastly, never wavering. Thank you for helping me fulfill my dreams and calling. Thank you for doing whatever it takes to be the best husband you can be, loving completely-holding nothing back, cuddling often (fulfilling my need for meaningful touch) and honoring me every day of the year. I know the Bible says that I am your helpmate, but you have been mine in countless ways. You never cease to amaze me, how you do all of my housework in a day, just so I don't have to. Thank you for making me laugh and being there for me when I cry. Thank you for sharing your gift of the Father with me, your passion for life, love, and wisdom. *The Love Legacy* series would not have been possible if it were not for your willingness to sacrifice for me, cheering me on, encouraging me, and sometimes pushing me beyond what I thought I could do or handle. You are an amazing, Christ-centered man, and I will tell every man within ear shot – "If you want to learn how to love your wife like Jesus loves His bride and have deep, fulfilling and lasting intimacy with her, then be mentored by Melvin (Red) Voyles, because this man knows how."

Thank You

Thank you, Jenene, Floyd, and Christine, my amazing publishing team. I could not have done this without you. Thank you for your patience, teaching, coaching, and excellence in your work. *The Love Legacy* series is touching lives, thanks to you!

Jesus, I save you for last because you are the center of my world and my foundation; without your healing, gifting, teaching, love, goodness and grace, nothing would be possible in my life. You have definitely turned my ashes into beauty and my mourning to joy. Thank you, my Savior, Lord, and Best Friend. Thank you for choosing to use my life to minister your healing to others. May you use the pain I have experienced to transform the lives of the readers who choose to pick up these books, for your good and glory. Hallelujah! Amen!

My Heart

My heart is to encourage others to fulfill their dreams by giving them the life skills (spirit, soul and body) that they need to succeed, propelling them forward to accomplish their God-given destiny to be, do, and have that for which they are created. I want to show my grandchildren that nothing is impossible with Jesus and their dreams are worthy of their best effort.

Proverbs 13:12 says, "*Hope deferred makes the heart sick:*
but when the desire comes, *it is a **tree of life**.*"

The miombo deep in the woodlands of Africa look much like the oak
trees in Alabama. The abundance species of these plants provide
natural resources for the native people, including firewood, charcoal,
timber, thatching grass, medicines, fruit and honey.

Chapter One
COURTROOM JEEBIES

You could have heard a pin drop in the stillness of the courtroom; the air was thick with the tension of a tight rope spread across a canyon. It was suffocating, like an Arizona monsoon. Maria could barely breathe. She felt as if she had been holding her breath for months now. Larry and Adaline's death had left a hole in their family's heart, and their little boy was the only thing that brought peace to the devastating intensity of the loss. Their lawyer felt they were sure to win temporary custody of the boy, but this did not help Maria and Brian's anxiety. Adaline's parents, Beatrice and Frederick, had promised to do whatever was necessary to obtain custody of the child.

The judge questioned both parties for about an hour and then called for a ten-minute recess. Maria went to the bathroom to collect herself and throw water on her face. Beatrice must have had the same idea and nearly knocked Maria down as she pushed past her. Although Maria seriously doubted that Beatrice would ruin her make-up by throwing water on her face; she could see the strain on her complexion and kind of felt sorry for her.

"I'm really sorry. We are trying to do what is right." Maria looked at her. A shiver went up her spine.

Beatrice's face was cold and rigid like it was frozen in place. She ignored Maria's comment, walked out and slammed the door behind her.

Brian paced back and forth down the cold brick hall. "Larry, I miss you. I need wisdom. I have a war raging inside of me. Do we have the right to keep your child? Don't get me wrong; we loved him from the moment he was placed in our arms. Is it right?" he whispered under his breath.

"Hon, come back in. The judge is ready," Maria called out.

"Mr. and Mrs. Frigmann, I realize this is your first appeal to the courts. You now have Joshua in your custody, correct?" the judge questioned.

"Yes, sir. We love the boy and are trying to fulfill his parents' wishes," Brian responded.

"After further investigation of this case, as requested by this couple's attorney, I order temporary custody of Joshua Aaron Ryan to Brian and Maria Frigmann. However, unsupervised visitation rights on a weekly basis will go to the grandparents of the child. You have all suffered a great loss, but none more than this child. Both couples will take parenting classes and go to grief counseling. My desire is to do what is best for this child. I will re-evaluate the case in six months," the judge stated.

"No! It's not fair. He is our grandchild, our daughter's son! How could you be so cold as to give him to strangers?" Beatrice blurted out.

"Beatrice!" Frederick reprimanded.

The judge looked at her compassionately. "Ma'am, I understand and am sorry for your loss, but I have read your daughter's will. It is my understanding that Brian and Maria were not strangers, but close friends. Let me advise you to spend as much time as you can getting to know your grandson. Follow my instructions, and I will see you again in six months. If there are any issues that cannot be resolved, make an appointment with my secretary. Good day."

"Yes, sir," Frederick replied. He lightly draped his arm around his wife. "Honey, it will be okay. This is just the beginning. Think of it as a preliminary before the big race. They haven't won. We are just warming up." He looked coldly at Brian. "We will be by on Friday at 6:00 p.m. to see our grandson," he demanded.

Beatrice threw his arm off her shoulder and stormed out the door.

"Okay, we'll put our calendars together then to see what works best for our families. Call any time to check on him. You can also Skype Maria on her cell phone. We want you to have time with Joshua. Did you know his name means 'Jehovah is generous?'" Brian replied, trying to lighten the conversation.

"Great! See you on Friday," Frederick responded.

They walked out the door. Maria sat in the corner crying.

"Honey, what's the matter? We won, for now. It'll be okay," Brian consoled.

"That woman is vicious. How am I supposed to correlate schedules and work with her?"

"She is grieving and angry. Adaline was their only child. You know how that feels. We need to show them compassion. I know it hurts. We are both hurting too, but they won't see that. May Jesus give us strength, help us see with His eyes, and love with his heart. Joshua needs them too," Brian spoke softly.

"I know. It's hard sometimes. I feel angry myself. I've been snappy to Angel. Poor thing. I think the counseling will do us all good." Maria grabbed Brian's hand. "Let's go get our kids. I'm sure Angel hasn't stopped talking since we left. Barbie is probably worn out."

As soon as they walked out the huge wooden doors, Maria's phone rang.

"Hi, yes, we did. Okay, we'll be there for supper at 6:00, but remember we'll head home tonight. Brian has the weekend shift at the hospital. I'm glad you're in town too, Mom. Thanks." Maria hung up.

Brian looked at her sternly. "We said we were going home after we picked up Angel and Joshua."

"I know, but my parents have been traveling a lot lately, and we've barely seen them in weeks. Angel asks to see them almost every day.

They want to celebrate with us. Oh, come on. Don't give me the dreaded furrowed brow. We would have to stop and eat anyway." She poked him in the rib.

Brian took her hand, led her to a bench just outside the courthouse, and sat down.

"We shouldn't be celebrating while the grandparents are mourning. You know this is temporary. We haven't won anything yet. It's six months. All it does is give more time for our hearts to be even deeper bonded with his, and then what?" Brian looked away.

"I know this is not what we want and could get super ugly, but for now, can we live today? Remember what Pastor Stroke preached Sunday about being mindful? We could drive ourselves crazy thinking about all the what-if's. They may never happen, and if they do, Jesus will see us through. Okay?" She pulled his face into her hands, kissed him, and held him close to her.

"I know you're right. I'll try. You drive. I need to rest a few minutes before we get our little Comanches," Brian responded.

At dawn Maria opened up the curtains in her living room and kitchen. The clear sky went from deep ocean blue to white and grey stratus clouds interwoven with cumulus clouds within a matter of hours. They looked as if they were having a battle as to who would win the atmosphere. In Maria's eyes it paralleled what was happening in their own home. The clouds slowly made their way trying to cover the sunlight that played peekaboo from behind them. The last few days had let loose a torrent of emotions.

Brian was wound up tight like a ball of string from working too many hours and the looming court battle over Joshua. The ridiculous antics of Beatrice and her constant criticisms didn't help. Plus, the pressure from the hospital board to relinquish the continued medical research on the Neatorama flower was exhausting and disheartening. He was running out of funding and time.

His words and actions were sharp, yet he wanted her to hold him close so he could bury his head in her chest to make all the tension go away. Minutes later the pent-up frustration would bubble to the surface again. The counseling classes had done little to ease his grief over losing his best friend.

Maria called her mom. "Mom, there is no way I can fix this for him, but I do what I can to make it better. I send him away to the coffee shop for quiet time while I prepare the carrot juice, make a salad, and prep for the week ahead, all while taking care of the children. Joshua and Angel are sensing it. They have both been fussy. I pray as I work that Jesus gives him peace. There are many emotions we both have to face from the last several months. He was the encourager at the beginning, but now I am. I don't know how to help him."

"Sweetie, it sounds like you are doing what you can. I have an idea. Why don't you see what day he has off, and I will come look after the kids? Y'all can take a day trip and go somewhere," Eula encouraged.

"Oh, Mom, that would be wonderful, but what about Beatrice?" Maria questioned.

"I can handle her; besides, she likes me," Eula retorted. "You could even bring them here; that would save Beatrice and Frederick from driving there."

"That is true. Okay. Got to go. Baby is crying. I think he is starting to teethe. Love you."

She let Eula talk to Angel. "Hang up when you are done, sweetie."

Chapter Two
HUMMINGBIRD PARADISE

As Brian and Maria made their way down the curvy mountain pass, the tree like columnar saguaro dotted the landscape, standing proud and tall. Velvet mesquite bushes were mixed among the boulders with their cream to yellow colored flowers, looking more like a pod of seeds. Creeping down further into a valley area, Palo Verde trees blossomed with bright yellow flowers.

Maria marveled that there would even be a museum this far from anywhere. She thought maybe their GPS was wrong, and they were lost in no man's land. However, there were several vehicles taking the slow path downward. Her heart breathed a sigh of relief when they finally saw signs confirming they were headed in the right direction.

"Wow, there it is. The Arizona Sonoran Desert Museum. It's bigger than I thought," Brian stated.

"Yes, I'm glad we brought plenty of water. Mom said our tickets would be waiting for us at the information booth. Their treat to us," Maria said.

"Nice!" Brian's excitement was like when Joshua use to drink a bottle. Maria had never seen a child so eager to eat. He would latch onto it with both hands and suck vigorously then giggle when he was full.

Maria laughed. "I'm glad to see you happy."

Brian collected their passes while Maria found a bathroom. Then they met up at the people counter.

"Okay, this trail of pavement goes in and out throughout the museum, but the other dust trail meanders its way to different areas of interest, like the hummingbird habitation. It appears to be like the butterfly area at the Phoenix Zoo. Do you want to go there first?" Brian asked.

"Yes, that sounds great! You have the map, and you are a better navigator, so I will follow you anywhere you go," Maria playfully countered.

"Is that right?" He pulled her to himself and kissed her passionately. "I would like to be at the birds of prey presentation at 12:15, so maybe we can see this exhibit and the art display before heading over to that area."

The chains and solid doors on the hummingbird exhibit allowed no room for escape. The place was filled with dense greenery, bright orange and yellow blooms, along with the smallest hummingbird feeders they had ever seen. They looked more like votive holders than feeders. The hummingbirds would dart about and land inches from the bystanders. The ruby-breasted, blue, and tiny black ones were exquisite to behold. Maria's camera clicked non-stop.

Maria expressed to Brian, "I am so thankful Mom could watch the children. We needed this break before the hearing."

Brian was lost in his own thoughts as he gazed out at the scenery. His heart was breaking at the thought of losing Joshua. It had been a brutal year of battling, and Brian was beginning to think it was not fair to any of them, especially to the boy. Adaline's parents made it clear they would only see him as the court ordered, or possibly not at all if they received the full custody they were seeking. Their lawyer was fighting tenaciously for their rights as the only blood relatives of the child. The first six months had been extended for another six after the sudden death of the assigned judge, and the case was then moved to Flagstaff due to the child's birth and residency there. He did not know how much more heartache he or Maria could take. Their children kept them sane. He looked over at his wife starring deep into a bush.

As Maria looked at the intricate markings of green, red, and blue on this tiny creature; it reminded her of the detail of her loving Heavenly Father. The wings took flight and soared next to Maria's ear, landing on her bright red shirt. She stood deathly still, not even wanting to breathe.

Unbeknownst to her, Brian stood a few feet away shooting pictures on his cell phone. The sound of its wings in flight gave Maria permission to exhale.

"Yippee Kiyah! What a sight to see!" Brian exclaimed.

"You got it?" Maria questioned.

"Yes, on picture and video. Wait until we show Angel. She will want to come next week."

She threw her arms around him. "I needed that. It's like Daddy said, 'It's going to be okay. I see every detail of what you are going through and I care deeply," Maria replied.

"Isn't it amazing that a camera can capture the wonder of creation, but it can't create it? No matter how desperately people may try to imitate God, they can't come close. They can create to some extent because the creator has given them that ability. Say this habitat for instance, man created it, but he did not create the birds, flowers, or vegetation. This is good, real good. It helps remind me who is in control, and I'm sure glad it's not me," Brian said as they sat on a bench peering at the beauty surrounding them.

Little droplets of water trickled down Maria's shirt. "What?" She looked up and above her head was another hummingbird. "Ooh, gross. Okay that is enough for me." She grabbed a towelette out of her bag and handed it to Brian. "Wipe down my back, please."

"Here? Now?" He cocked one eyebrow up.

"Yes, come on." Maria begged. "I'm glad you think this is funny. Women don't like pee down their backs."

Brian opened his water bottle and poured a little down her back, then soaked it up with the cloth.

"Let's go get a drink before the bird show. I saw a coffee shop in the gift store," Brian responded.

He was thankful this year had only drawn them closer without pulling them apart. He grabbed her hand and squeezed tightly, their silent affirmation of love.

After having a light snack, they made their way back to the presentation. The two handlers were wearing khaki pants and vests with lots of pockets and tan Aussie hats. Gray Hawks with black-tipped feathers whizzed past everyone's heads. Brian and Maria could almost feel the brush of their wings as they soared upwards. The white owls were extraordinary, flying close enough to touch, their plush calamus, the color of a bleached cloth. The red-tailed hawk increased in altitude until he was barely visible, then spiraled down, quickly landing on the handler's arm to eat its reward. We were enthralled with these creatures and surprised they were completely untethered. In fact, we did not think the Peregrine Falcon was going to return, but it did. The handler said this bird could sweep down 200 miles per hour when pursuing prey. These gorgeous creatures inhabited this region and sometimes did not return, but most knew where their food source was and did.

The handlers did a fabulous display. Someone in the audience asked the overseer why the Sonoran Desert had such a vast display of plants and wildlife. He answered by saying the Sonoran Desert was the lushest desert on earth because the Pacific Northwest winter storms left gentle winter rains, and the Gulf of California's summer monsoons sent seasonal wind patterns, along with wet, tropical air, that produced violent thunderstorms.

Maria would not go into the snake habitat with Brian. She said they gave her the creepy-crawlies, and she had enough of that lately. Instead, she made her way over to the art exhibit. The display included some local young artists, and she recognized a friend's son's name. The artwork was a cougar's head nicely drawn to scale. She took a picture of it to show Brian.

They agreed to meet back at the outdoor snack bar to eat. Maria decided to call her mom and check on the kids. They had swum in the kiddie pool and were now napping. After talking to her mom, she sat lost in her thoughts and almost did not hear her phone ringing. Brian came up behind her and kissed her neck.

"Babe, you going to get that? You okay?" Brian asked.

She fumbled in her brown leather backpack purse, but it was too late.

"Oh well, maybe they'll leave a message. I don't recognize the number anyway. Next time I buy one of these purses, remind me to get one that has a phone pouch," Maria sighed.

"Sure, but you usually don't go purse shopping with me." He laughed.

Maria listened to her message on speaker. "This is Mrs. Doughty from Keenly Adoption Agency. I would like to speak to you right away. It's urgent. Please, call my office to set up an appointment as soon as possible. Thank you."

"Wow. What do you think of that?" Maria asked.

"I think we are in the middle of a custody battle for Joshua. They have impeccable timing; that's for sure," he replied.

"It can't hurt to meet with her," Maria countered with tear-filled eyes. "We may eventually lose Angel and Joshua. Please."

"Okay. You win. God is in control."

They met with the adoption agency that evening. There was a need for immediate placement for a set of infant twins whose mom had been addicted to cocaine. They were premature, and one was sickly. The courts took them from the hospital as soon as they were stable; no one wanted them.

Brian sat frozen in his chair. "Twins? Twins?" His mind toyed with him. He was thinking of all the scenarios that could go wrong with this placement when Mrs. Doughty interrupted his thoughts.

"Look, I know this is a lot to take in, but I think they would make a good fit for you. Do you want to meet them at least?" She pulled some pictures from her briefcase. "This is Allon, a little boy. His name means, 'Strong as an oak,' and this is Abbie, which means, 'My Father rejoices.' The nurses at St. Josephs' chose those names for the children, but when the adoption goes through you can change them."

"The boy looks so tiny. Is he okay?" Maria replied.

Brian stared in disbelief. He looked at the pictures and their names. "They are fragile and helpless. May we have a minute?"

"Most certainly," she said as she stepped out of the room.

"Honey, this is happening way too fast," Brian told Maria.

"I know, look at them. Remember the first time we saw Joshua in the crib, all alone in that nursery? Our hearts melted, and we knew he was ours. You are a pediatrician. What a great home for two premature, drug-addicted infants who need specialized care," Maria consoled.

"But I'm afraid it will be too much for you, a kindergartener, a one year old, and now twins barely four weeks old?" Brian shook his head.

"I can hire Alesha to help out on the days you work. She can do her classwork between their naps and feedings. I'm sure within a short time I can handle it on my own. I'm kind of gifted that way. God brought her into our life for such a time as this. He's been preparing her from the first time we ministered to her in that coffee shop. I knew she had a way with children when she held Angel the first time. Since she's going to be a PA in pediatrics, it will be good experience for her," Maria responded.

He looked into her pleading eyes, leaned in, and kissed her. "Let's pray."

After he prayed, he stuck his head out and asked the adoption counselor to come back in.

"We've decided to give it a try. When will we get them?" Brian asked.

"There is still some paperwork that needs to be done, but the CPS worker will bring them to your home. She will call you. The nurses donated a lot of baby stuff and have set up a fund in their names. You will have full access to it for whatever you need for the babies. We also have some resources for you. I know you are not new to the adoption process, but let's go over the details one more time. If you have any questions, problems, or uncertainties, please do not hesitate to call me. I actually have twins and would be glad to help in any way I can," she explained.

Chapter Three
RESCUED FROM JAWS OF DEATH

Smoke rose from the valley below. The barely visible inner huts were ablaze, and the orange-red flames licked the sky. Screeches filled the darkness. Chaos ensued. The white painted faces of warriors with bows drawn tight and piercing arrows in place etched their way through the brush, crouching like a lioness about to pounce on her prey. The search party located Angel's biological father and sent up flairs. The chief's son remained prisoner after being captured years prior. Rojomen's spies sent word that he was alive. They were there to set him free.

Three men had been sent ahead to start fires as a distraction to lure them from the captive's thatched hut. Rojomen ordered his spies to kill anyone who stood between them and the rescue of their master, but only if absolutely necessary. His desire was for peace between their people. Most of the men from this tribe were gone on a hunting party and only a few were left behind to guard.

The men scattered as Rojomen went to the east with two of his men. He slowly eased upon the hut and signaled for the other men to split to the sides. They would keep watch. He carefully raised the edge of the tent flap, poking his spear through first followed by his head. He brought his hand to his mouth signaling the lady inside not to make a sound. In hushed tones he spoke to her in their native tongue.

"I won't harm you. Tell me where the captives are," he insisted.

She pointed to the middle of the dirt floor. Rojomen used the tip of his spear to gently pull back the edge of the woven rug. Underneath was a hole covered by a board. A faint groan came from the small opening.

"Sit!" He ordered the woman.

She obeyed without hesitation.

Rojomen could hear a ruckus outside, but he stayed focus on his mission. He threw the board and rug aside. The hole was too small for his large frame. He lay on his stomach, reaching his long arms through the opening. His heart beat with anticipation and the knowledge of his vulnerability at being in this position. He kept a watchful eye on the young lady whose eyes were filled with fear. He could tell by her elongated legs and round cheeks that she was not from this tribe. His hands brushed against something.

"Master, Master," he called. Rojomen grabbed frantically, trying to latch on to the object. He was sure it was a body, but he could not see in the darkness of the hole. Time was running out.

"Master, can you move? Scoot to me," he whispered.

Silence, stench, nothingness. Rojomen bowed his head and prayed. "Father, help me."

He grabbed what felt like an arm. He pulled it toward him. Then he felt a torso and tried to get his hands underneath it, but he could not. He called the lady over.

"You are small enough. Grab him. I'll pull you both up; I am strong," he pleaded.

He could hear more screaming and scuffling outside the tent hut.

"Hurry, please! I promise I'll let you go," he urged.

She could not resist the desperation and tenderness in his eyes. There was something different about this man. She got on her knees, and Rojomen held her legs as he lowered her upper body through the hole.

"Wrap your arms around his chest," he said.

She yelled, "Death! Death!"

"No, do it now!" he commanded. The woman obeyed his order. He yanked with all of his strength. His heart sank at the thin, limp body held in the lady's arms. Only his groin was covered, his ribs poked through his skin, and his body was covered with sores and mites. His lips parched and swollen.

"Oh, Master." He breathed. He turned to the lady who had crawled out from under the man and said, "Thank you."

He wrapped the barely breathing body softly in the blankets as the woman kindly helped. Her eyes were soft with compassion now. The noise outside had quieted. He threw his master over his shoulder.

"He is not dead. He will live. We have miracle medicine," Rojomen spoke.

The woman followed him. "No, you stay," he said gently.

"I come with you!" she said defiantly.

Rojomen did not have time to argue. He chose not to go through the front opening as he did not know what awaited them. He used his machete and cut a triangular escape route, carefully easing his head out to make sure the path was clear. A shadow in the dark made its way toward them. He gently laid his master next to the tree and softly pushed the woman toward him, but as the figure approached, he could see it was one of his men. He relayed that the warriors had subdued the other men in the village, tied them up, and put out the fires.

All of his men had escaped, and the others eyed the lady suspiciously, but no one questioned Rojomen's authority.

Once they were out of harm's way, they lay the half-dead body of the rescued man on the ground and circled around him. The medicine man took a pouch of precious ointment and rubbed it on his head, chest, and sores. Then they prayed to the God of Heaven.

Chapter Four
CHRISTMAS TREE MEMORIES

The Christmas tree dazzled with shimmering white needles from the glory of the pure driven snow weighing down its branches. As the sun danced across its magnificent limbs, they sparkled like diamonds. Brian marveled at the symbolism of purity all around him. No footprints tainted the ground. He realized this must be what a soul made new looks like.

He wrestled intensely with the Lord this year. It had come with tremendous blessing, but at the cost of one of his most valued relationships. Larry, his best friend, had been happier than Brian had ever seen him. He and his wife, Adaline, were expecting their first child. Then it was all stripped away so suddenly; it was hard to comprehend. The wreckage left a fight Brian did not want nor had he anticipated.

However, the little boy he rocked to sleep when he was home at night filled his heart. He wondered how life could be taken away and yet given. Then he thought of the reason he was in the forest on a freezing morning.

As Brian sawed the pine trunk he prayed, "Yes, Lord, it is about your son. He gave his life to give us ours. I understand. Thank you for your forgiveness, cleansing, and healing. If you want us to keep the twins, Joshua and Angel, you will make a way. They are precious gifts on loan to us for however long you deem them so. Help me say that prayer every day and be submissive to your will. Help Maria and me be okay, come what may. Thank you for your strength. Now, let's get this tree home."

This tree would be placed on their front porch as in years past, letting all of the neighbors enjoy it. In the evening the red and white lights carried a lustrous glow. The night was lit up by a single star and an old plastic manger scene handed down from Brian's grandparents. It was still the center of their Christmas and a sweet reminder of years he spent as a child on the farm.

Oh, the stories his grandpa could tell. His grandma would punch him on the shoulder and laugh. Brian could hear the echo of her words in his head, "Don't fill that boy's head with such nonsense."

The memories were bittersweet. As Brian touched the head of Mary he could picture the oak coffin being lowered into the ground. His grandmother passed away on Christmas Eve when he was ten, and his grandfather passed on Christmas Day the following year. People said his grandfather died of a broken heart; Brian knew this was true. He saw how deeply they loved each other. He laughed as he reflected on how different they were, as different as night and day. His Papa was a hard-working, fun-loving jokester. His grandma was sweet, and a little too serious sometimes, kept everything in order. They balanced each other out.

As Brian stood on his front lawn pondering these thoughts, he heard a sweet voice. "Daddy, what are you thinking about?" Angel crept softly onto the front porch.

He bounded up the steps and sat down in the rocker, "Come here and I will tell you." The five-year-old climbed up in her daddy's lap.

"My Papa taught my grandma how to have fun and enjoy life. They were both godly examples to me, just like Mema and Papa are to you."

"What does that mean?" she asked.

"Well, remember last week when you told your mom that you did not have cake at Mema's house?" he questioned.

"Yes," she said sheepishly.

"Your Mema called and encouraged you to tell the truth. That is a godly example," he explained.

"I understand. Tell me more, please," she pleaded.

"I learned a lot of lessons over the campfire. Papa loved to camp, and even when we didn't go to the woods, we built a fire in his back yard. We roasted marshmallows. On the farm he taught me how to throw hay and clean up the horse corrals," he continued.

"Woo, gross. That doesn't sound fun!" she exclaimed.

"But for a young boy it was. It made me strong. I worked beside Grandma in the kitchen, baking, washing dishes, setting the table, and the best part is she taught me how to fish. She loved fishing. Whether I was stacking wood or working in the house, the lessons they taught me were invaluable."

"What does 'invaluable' mean?"

"You know how much you love Doggie, right?" She shook her head yes as she squeezed her stuffed dog tightly.

"Well, if I said I would buy you a new dog, and we could just throw Doggie in the trash, would that be okay?"

"No!"

"Why? Because you love him and he means a lot to you. You wouldn't trade him for a new doggy because he is invaluable or can't be replaced. Does that make sense?"

"Yes! Thanks Daddy." She climbed down from his lap.

"Off to bed now. I'll be in shortly." He kissed her on the cheek.

He went back to his thoughts of hard work, family, friendship, marriage, integrity, fun, and the love his grandparents taught him. He was sorry that his children could not benefit from their presence, but he was grateful for the godly heritage they left. He prayed he could pass down their legacy through his own life, a testament to them and the Jesus they loved.

Eula sat in her comfy rose recliner wrapped in the soft fleece blanket Brian and Maria gave her for Christmas. She never remembered the valley being this cold. Aaron left early to meet some brothers for coffee and Bible study. She basked in the quiet of the morning.

The bustle of the holidays was over, and for the first time in weeks, her home was quiet and without guests. The Christmas decorations were packed away, and she missed the smiling snowmen. She had over thirty of them, ranging in every size; most were gifts from the people she loved, and a few were snowmen she had picked up at after-Christmas sales. They made her heart sing.

She was not sure why she liked them, but they sure made her smile, laugh, and dance around like a child, especially when Angel pressed all of the musical ones at the same time. As her eyes made their way around the room, she stopped midair and stared in disbelief. On top of the bookshelf sat a lonely snowman, his once twelve-inch frame a mere eight inches now. This one was a once-fragrant ornament which shrunk with time. His shiny toboggan, carrot nose, and face shone with a look of bewilderment. He was soft-looking, but the eyes made you question if he was thinking, "Why am I fading away?"

It was comical and ingenious for someone to think of creating a shrinking snowman. He faded away over time in essence like a real snowman. Eula laughed as she picked up her "Good Morning, Beautiful" coffee mug.

"What are you trying to say to me this morning, Lord? You sure have a sense of humor," she whispered.

Eula walked out on the front porch. The dazzling orange red ball appeared just above the horizon of the Superstition Mountains with thick, bubbly, white clouds threatening to engulf it and drown out its glorious beauty.

"Hmmm, the weather didn't say anything about a winter storm today," she commented.

"But we sure could use the rain!" the postman hollered from the mailbox.

"You're right. Have a blessed day," she replied.

She pulled her coat up around her neck and sat on her swing watching the scenery before her. The birds were fluttering about, obviously trying to stay warm, she reasoned. The frenzy landed high above her head on the rooftop T.V. antenna. Their beaks went from side to side as if they were having a conversation with each other. The male was solid black, except for a touch of white and red on his wings. His obnoxiously loud chirp overpowered the female's. Maybe they were seeking a good place to build a nest come spring. They both looked at the lemon and grapefruit trees. Eula thought these seemed like viable options, but the female bird started wildly chirping as if to say, "No, the grapefruit branches are too clustered together." She suddenly flew over to the lemon tree as if to make her point known, "This is perfect. The limbs are cut high above the ground. They are full enough to build a nest, but not too dense, and the fruit will provide nourishment."

Eula laughed, "I need to write children's books. My imagination is out of this world."

Chapter Five
SWEET IRONY

The historic Arizona red sandstone brick building stood out against the aqua sky. Its towering square clock tower and steeple made it look like an old church building, instead of a Romanesque Revival-style courthouse. The structure was built in 1894 with arched windows and large windows and doors. It could be welcoming or scary, depending on your proximity to it.

Despite Beatrice and Frederick's appeal to have the hearing moved to Maricopa County, the judge ordered it to be held in the county of the child's birth at the Coconino County Courthouse in Flagstaff. It was nothing like the modern buildings in other parts of the county. It stood tall against the mountain greenery behind it.

Brian and Maria walked hand in hand toward the entryway, making their way into the courthouse and down the long hall to the judge's corridor. They were apprehensive about the hearing, which would determine final custody of Joshua. She was shaking. Brian pulled her to the side of the hall and held her close. Maria cried all morning while dressing the child. Her eyes were red and swollen. Barbie, Eula, and Aaron took the children to the nearby park to play. Brian felt it would be too demanding on them to deal with everyone's emotions on top of their own. If the judge awarded full custody to Adaline's parents, Aaron would bring Joshua after the hearing.

"Honey, it will be okay. We have to trust. I know it's hard; my stomach is in knots, but we will make it through together. I love you," he said as he put his hands on each side of her face and turned it toward him. He kissed her on the forehead. "We will be okay. I promise."

As they waited on the wooden bench outside the courtroom, Maria's thoughts wandered to the last conversation she had with Beatrice. Adaline's heart would be broken if she knew the battle they had fought with the "grandparent's rights" laws. Their desire was never to inhibit the grandparents from being a part of the child's life. Their only wish was to carry out Larry and Adaline's request, to follow through with the promise made by Brian on Adaline's deathbed. Tears welled up in her eyes, and Brian squeezed her hand a little tighter.

Joshua Aaron was a shining light in this deep, dark tunnel they muddled through. His bright blue eyes sparkled with Larry's color, and his plump, rosy cheeks matched Adaline's facial features. He was the perfect mixture of his parents.

Beatrice sat on the cold, brick wall, puffing on a cigarette on the smoker's patio. Her heart was frigid as one single tear fell down her cheek. The hearing was in less than an hour, but she could not help wondering if this was all a mistake. She had never put any child's needs above her own, not even Adaline's. Frederick had changed since their daughter's death; he had always wanted a son, and he saw Joshua as a chance to make things right.

She stared out in the distance, thinking of a time when life seemed simpler, before her grandparents' inheritance spoiled their lives.

She frolicked in the tall grass in the field next to her grandmother's rose gardens. Her chubby little hands picked the yellow daisies. The skies were filled with children's laughter, as her older sister and brothers played hide-n-seek amongst the pecan grove. This was the most vivid and precious memory she had as a child. Her grandmother would sit and tell them Bible stories for hours, making them come alive with her animal, people, and nature animations. They never grew bored and would act out the stories she told.

As suddenly as this memory came, the dark cloud followed, driving it away. Beatrice stiffened, not allowing any further memories to filter in. The icy talons of fear and death normally sent her searching for a drink, the only thing that would keep the horrific memories at bay and the pain buried.

A midnight blue hummer rumbled its way into the gravel parking lot of the small Flagstaff children's park. Barbie let out a squeal.

"What in the world?" Aaron shouted.

She turned and looked over her shoulder. "Boyfriend." She winked.

Eula cackled as she watched Joshua climb up the stairs to the toddler slide. "He is getting good at this."

"That wind is a little nippy. Do you think I should put the twins back in the car?" Aaron asked.

"Yes," Eula replied. "Do you know what time Angel needs to be picked up from school?"

Barbie walked up with her friend. "I will pick her up early today. Maria wants her here when the hearing is over. Let me introduce you to my boyfriend, Ken."

Ken extended his hand. "It is a pleasure to meet you. I've heard so much about you."

"I wish we could say the same." Aaron patted him on the arm. "Just kidding. Nice to meet you too. Don't mind me; I'm protective of my girls."

Barbie's phone rang. "Shhh. It's Maria. Hello. Yes, we will. It is time to pray; they are going into the courtroom."

Aaron wheeled the stroller in the middle of the circle and picked up Joshua, holding him close. They all joined hands and prayed until the infants started to cry.

"They're hungry. Want to help me feed them in the car?" Eula asked Barbie as she dabbed her eyes. "You guys watch Joshua!" she hollered to the men.

"Sure. I have about thirty minutes before we go get Angel," Barbie responded.

"You take Abbie then. She's a guzzler. You can't feed her fast enough, burp her good or she'll spit up on you," Eula countered.

As they sat in the car, Eula asked Barbie where she met Ken.

"You know I am going for my degree as a nurse practitioner, right?"

Eula nodded her head.

"He is one of the doctors on staff at the hospital where I have been doing rotations. He is kind, funny, protective, but not controlling. We both have extremely busy schedules, but he makes time for me. Most importantly, he loves Jesus and has good relationships with his mother and sisters. He has six sisters and two brothers; he's right dab in the middle of them. They are a close-knit family. After my last boyfriend broke up with me because of my Lyme's disease, I didn't want to introduce Ken to my family until I was sure about our relationship."

"You know, we are happy for you. I'm glad he came today. We all need the extra support, and he seems genuine," Eula responded.

Frederick poked his head out the door, "Please, come in. They are about ready. Are you okay?"

"I will be when this is over, and we can get on with our lives." She pushed past him.

The court attendant came out and told them, "You may come in; the judge is ready for you now."

They filed in; Maria and Brian to the left, Beatrice and Frederick to the right with their respective lawyers.

"All rise for the Honorable Judge Stewart," the attendant announced.

They all diligently obeyed.

A new judge sat on the bench. She was tall and thin. Her ebony eyes were filled with compassion and sincerity. She held her posture with dignity and pride.

"You may be seated. I have reviewed this case thoroughly and made my decision. Please allow me to completely finish what I have to say before you ask questions or ask for an appeal. Due to the laws that now govern this state, I must issue the custody decree to the grandparents of the child. However, in my jurisdiction I have certain rights, and since the child was born in a Flagstaff hospital, I am awarding partial custody to Brian and Maria. They will have the child two days or one weekend out of the month for the next year. Since the grandparents live in the valley, you will take turns delivering and returning the child. You can work these arrangements out among yourselves. I will review this case for final sign off in one year. At that time, it will be Beatrice and Frederick's decision whether or not you are a part of the child's life. It is my hope, for Joshua's sake, that you four will become friends. We all can learn from each other. Thank you. This hearing is adjourned."

"Oh my God. You've got to be kidding me!" Beatrice quipped.

Maria hugged Brian and cried. "At least we didn't lose him completely," she whimpered.

He walked over to shake the hands of the grandparents. Frederick politely extended his hand. Beatrice just stood there.

"Where is my grandson?" she demanded.

"He is at the park. Maria is calling them to bring him now," Brian responded. "Look, we are happy for you and want to work with you anyway we can."

"Thank you. I'm sure we will need it," Frederick commented.

"I'm waiting out in the hall." Beatrice walked off.

"She'll come around. Be patient with her. She loves the boy," Frederick defended.

"I know," Brian said sympathetically.

Not ten minutes later, Aaron brought Joshua in. He put him down, and the boy ran to Maria.

"Mommmmmmyyy!" he yelled, wrapping his little arms around Maria's legs.

She knelt down and hugged him close. "My sweet little one. I love you so much!" She pressed back the tears, not wanting to upset the child. "Look who's here to pick you up, Grandma and Grandpa."

The boy clung to Maria and buried his head into her shoulder. Beatrice walked over and pulled him away. He screamed and kicked.

"Joshua, it's okay," Maria tried to console. Tears streamed down her face.

Aaron jumped in, "Don't be rough. He doesn't like that. Be gentle with him; he has a sensitive spirit."

Beatrice and Frederick headed to the car. Brian ran to catch up with them. "Here are his toys and clothes." He was shaking, trying to maintain his composure.

Frederick reached out his hand to take the bag, but Beatrice knocked it away.

"We don't need those things. He has new belongings at our house," She smarted.

"At least let him have his bear; he won't sleep without it. Please, it was Adaline's," Brian pleaded.

Frederick handed the bear to the child and eyed Beatrice sternly. "Thank you." He took the boy and hugged him tight, then placed him in his car seat. He motioned for Brian to come over.

"I'm sorry. You can tell him bye. We'll bring him to you next Friday," he said.

Brian kissed Joshua on the head. "I love you to the moon and back. We'll see you real soon." He pulled himself away from the arms that clenched his shirt. His heart melted as he turned away.

The rest of the family waved from the courthouse steps. Eula was holding Maria. There was not a dry eye among them as they watched Beatrice and Frederick pull away with Joshua clinging to his little bear, tears streaming down his face.

Brian handed Maria the bag and fell into her arms. The family encircled them.

"Father, we thank you that this is not a loss. We still get to have the child. He has not been taken from us completely, and for that we are most grateful. We pray that through this year we will be able to be a light to Beatrice and Frederick. We pray they will come to know you and love that little boy the way you intend for them to. Thank you that they are honoring Adaline by raising the child and not hiring someone else to do it. Thank you that they have learned from their previous mistakes. We know they are scared, Lord. Make Beatrice's heart tender. Comfort our children during this difficult transition and give them the compassion they will need to handle every situation. Thank you for Angel and the twins. In Jesus' name, amen," Aaron prayed.

Barbie came up the courthouse walk. Angel ran to her mom and dad.

"Daddy, where's Joshua? I didn't get to say bye." She held her head down.

Brian picked her up and swung her into the air. "He'll be back soon."

Even though it was a short drive back to the house, it seemed like an eternity; both twins woke up crying. Angel kept asking questions Maria did not want to answer. Her parents had to leave as they were flying out for a speaking engagement. Barbie and Ken went to pick up lunch for all of them.

"Barbie and Ken, funny, huh?" Brian poked at Maria.

"I'm not in the mood." She looked at him forlornly.

"We have to focus on what we do have, not on what we don't. You'll drive yourself crazy. It hurts. I know; I hurt too. Anyone up for a hot chocolate?" he said, putting his mirror down to see Angel's eyes.

"Me! Daddy, Me!" she yelled.

"Inside voice. Babe, can't you hear the twins back there?" Maria confronted.

"They'll be okay. Look, there isn't even a line. It won't take five minutes. We need to celebrate a little. We get to see Joshua Friday. Yeah! Thank you, Jesus!" Brian pulled up to the window and placed their order. He handed Maria her Chai with coconut milk and cinnamon on the top and Angel her coconut milk with a splash of hazelnut.

"Thanks, you're right. This is good, not Bergies, but good." She took a cloth and wiped her face. "Let's sing "Jesus Loves Me," and maybe the twins will quiet down a little. They love to be sung to, just like you used to when you were a baby, Angel. Soft though, okay; don't bellow. Remember how Mommy taught you." Maria instructed.

Sure enough, the twins calmed down to Maria's soothing voice.

Chapter Six
LIFE RELIVED

Eula's palms were sweaty, and her heart beat wildly as she took to the podium. Aaron traveled across the country sharing the testimony of his life, illness, death, and healing. But rarely had he asked Eula to speak about how this had affected her. He knew she did not like to be in the limelight.

"Good morning. May I open with prayer?" It was more of a statement than a request, presented to the roughly three hundred people in the audience. She scanned the crowd and felt comfortable proceeding. "Heavenly Father, you know I'm not a speaker. Thank you that it's not about my ability, but my availability to be used by you that brings me here. May the words I speak tonight minister life to someone in Jesus' name."

She took a sip of water and smiled at the audience.

"Life is full of joys, laughter, sorrow, and tears. It is during the tough times that we discover who we are and what we are made of. We learn how deeply we love. The struggles of this life build, mold, and shape us. They only define who we are, if we allow them to. They could pull apart our relationship with God and others.

Aaron and I have been married almost forty years. We were high school sweethearts. The first several years were rocky, more like earthquatic, if that was a word."

Laughter filled the room and helped ease Eula's nerves. She continued, "Our daughter, Maria, pushed, prodded, and begged us every, and I mean every, Sunday to go to church with her. She was extremely involved in a youth group with her best friend, Nicole. Finally, one Christmas we went to watch her perform in a pageant, but this year was different than the others. Our daughter bravely sang one of the most beautiful renditions of "Silent Night" that we had ever heard with tears coursing down her cheeks. You see, she and Nicole rehearsed over and over again, hoping Nicole would make it to the pageant, but she died of cancer only a few days before. This changed us forever; at the end of the service we allowed Maria to lead us in a prayer to accept Jesus into our hearts and make Him Lord.

I say all of that because without Him, Aaron and I probably wouldn't be together. My plan was to leave after Maria graduated high school. I didn't know there was any other way, but Jesus changed us. We started working on our marriage and went to a godly counselor. We learned what love and intimacy truly meant, as well as the source of it. Other couples who mentored us taught us to rely on Jesus as our source, purpose, security, and identity. We stopped trying to get those needs filled from each other. There is no way I could have endured the events that followed those years without a firm foundation in Jesus and in our marriage.

As I sat in the cold, white, sterile hospital room of my husband's surgical recovery unit, the doctor gave the news no one wants to hear. "Your husband has stage four lung cancer." The doctor pointed to the film on the screen and explained there were multiple lesions in both of his lungs. We had to start an aggressive form of chemotherapy and radiation right away. The biopsies would confirm the diagnosis.

As I sat numb, holding Aaron's hand, rage coursed through me. I'd never felt such anger well up inside of me toward anything.

My husband asked about the prognosis with treatment.

The doctor told us it was a few months at best and that we would know more when the test results were in.

After the doctor left the room we held each other and cried. Our thoughts were, "How can this be happening? It's not fair. Why? What do we do? and after all the intimacy we've built into our marriage, we like being together. Not now, Lord, please." We learned to cast each emotion on Jesus as they would surface, but we worried about our daughter and her family. They had recently lost a child, adopted a little girl, and Maria was close to her father. Our hearts ached for her. We grieved deeply. We loved each other more than we ever had. The question of, "How could I go on without Aaron?" plagued my thoughts, along with how to tell our family. I tried to remain strong in my faith, but I questioned God. I screamed, yelled, and stomped my feet. I laid on the floor and pleaded for my husband's healing. I'm being honest with you, folks, laying it all on the table.

I fought depression and oppression, all while trying to hide it from the people I loved. I watched my husband go from a lean, mean, fighting machine to a weak, skin and bones man. After the biopsies confirmed the terminal diagnosis, we refused the treatment and sought alternative methods. We started juicing and changed our diets to be as pure as possible.

I finally got up the nerve to tell our children, which was the most challenging thing to do. We found a hospital in Mexico, Oasis of Hope, that used life-changing, natural alternatives to treat cancer. We flew there and stayed at the hospital. The doctors and staff were kind, but honest about Aaron's condition. It was grave. Even while in treatment there, he was coughing up blood. It was terrifying, and they promised no cure. They offered prayer, treatment, nutrition, and support. Many of their patients had been given less than a month to six months to live in the states, but there they were living good, quality lives, even though they weren't completely cancer-free. We felt good about the treatment we received there before returning home.

Aaron was weak, but his color returned, and he seemed better. We were hopeful. We made him comfortable at home and allowed him to do whatever he could do. We did everything we were told to do, but one evening he started gasping for air. We rushed him to the emergency room. They inserted the longest needle I'd ever seen into his back and withdrew two liters of yellowish, green fluid from his lungs.

When they were finished I excused myself and ran to the bathroom. I knelt on the cold, tile bathroom floor and cried out to God, "Jesus, heal my husband, or take him home. Enough is enough. I can't bear to see him suffer anymore."

"Code Blue" rang out over the intercom minutes later. They resuscitated him and moved him to ICU. Brian, Maria, and I surrounded his bed. Aaron was unconscious, and the doctor said he would not make it through the night. We sang his favorite hymns and prayed. He opened his eyes once, and as I looked into his face, he spoke volumes without saying a word; peace exuded from him. Then he took his last breath. The monitor blared around him, and the nurse came in to shut it off. The DNR was final. For five minutes we held him and each other. There was complete silence.

Then the monitor began to flicker, and there was a slight thump, thump, thump, thump of his heartbeat. The nurse rushed in, in disbelief; she immediately paged the doctor to the room.

I know this will be hard for you to believe, but my husband sat straight up on that bed and smiled. God breathed life back into his damaged lungs. He will tell you the rest of his story, but I'm here to testify that every word is true, and I'm a grateful woman. Jesus gave him back to me."

Eula's eyes filled with tears. Aaron came on stage, gave her a hug, and stood beside her.

"My wife is the most precious person in the world to me." He turned to her and said, "I love you."

He gave her a kiss, and she walked off the stage. Everyone in the auditorium was standing and applauding.

Eula felt exhilarated and exhausted all at the same time. "Thank you, Father."

The stage director, a young woman in her late thirties with long, dark hair streaked in purple and a thin smile, approached her and said, "Ma'am. Ma'am. You forgot your shawl."

"Oh, thank you," Eula responded.

"Your speech moved me deeply. I lost my mom suddenly to a stroke last year. We were extremely close. I moved her from another state to be with me here. I'd been busier than ever at work, and I didn't even realize she was sick. My dad was never there for me. They divorced when I was five, so it's been devastating to me. I've cried every day this year, longing for relationship, looking everywhere, but not finding it." Her lips began to quiver.

"Oh, hon, I'm sorry. May I give you a hug and pray for you?" Eula asked. She shook her head yes. Eula prayed the Lord would comfort her and minister his healing to her.

"Do you know Jesus? I mean do you have a personal relationship with him? I assumed because you do these events you do, but do you?" Eula questioned.

"No, I lied on the application because I needed the job. It's hard to understand why a good God would allow all these bad things to happen in my life. I have nobody. I work all of the time to make ends meet. By the way, I am Jody." She extended her hand to Eula.

"Jesus, can be your best friend. He will never leave you. I don't know why things happen the way they do, but I know He loves you and has a plan for your life. Would you like to ask him to forgive your sin and invite Him into your life?" Eula asked.

Someone yelled her name from the back end of the stage.

"I've got to take this out. I'll be right back." She ran a bottle of water and a chalk board out to the stage and positioned them appropriately. She moved the chalk and podium closer to the center of the stage, along with some other props, then returned. "I missed my que. Now, where were we?"

"I'm sorry. Do you want to invite Jesus into your life?" Eula replied.

"Yes, I do want to receive Jesus. I've listened to these speakers for months now, and I realized tonight how desperately I need Him." Jody bowed her head and repeated the prayer Eula cited to her.

"Here is my card. Call me anytime. Actually, would you like to join us for dinner?" Eula commented.

"I need to finish wrapping things up here. Then I would love to. Here is my number. Text me the address of the restaurant. I feel so good! Thank you." She hugged Maria and went about her work.

Aaron completed his speech, gave out Bibles, the material on Oasis of Hope, a monthly devotional he had put together, and prayed with a few people.

"You did a fantastic job tonight," he told Eula as they packed his teaching materials into the car. "Let's go eat; I'm famished."

"Oh no!" Aaron rolled over. "My alarm didn't go off."

Eula sighed, "Well, we are both late getting started today. It's okay. We got home late last night. Evidently we both needed the rest. The time with Jody made it well worth it."

She got up and made herself ready for the day, lingering in the shower and letting it wash all the tension away. Aaron made the bed, stuck his head in to kiss her goodbye, and headed for the gym. He had to get these workouts in when he could. His speaking engagements were picking up, some back to back.

Eula contemplated going straight for her quiet time and studies but knew her husband's needs were a priority too. She whispered, "Thank you, Lord for understanding. You know he has a full plate today, and this will bless him."

She washed all the fruit and veggies for the week, made a salad, and Aaron's snack packs with his favorite vegetables and hummus. As she packed his lunch for the day, she hummed one of her favorite songs, "Overcomer" by Mandisa. The phone rang. "Hello," she answered.

"Mom, help, please. Allon is spitting up, and I can't get him to stop. The pediatrician's office doesn't open for another hour, and Brian is observing a surgery today. We had this problem with Angel, and it scares me." Maria cried.

"Maria, first take a breath." She gave her a few seconds to do so and counted with her. "Now, tell me what he's had this morning. Does he have a fever?"

"No fever. He's had four ounces of formula twice today. I warmed it this time thinking it would help his belly, instead of adding the hot water from the machine. Do you think that could have done it? Why would it make a difference?"

"It shouldn't, but he is sensitive. He's been spitting up, right?" Eula asked.

"Yeah, but not like this. I can't tend to both babies and get Angel ready for school like this. Joshua is coming today too. I won't cancel time with him. I'm supposed to pick him up. Do you think you could bring him?"

"Listen. First, let's deal with problem one. You need to breathe. Allon handles water well, correct? Wait thirty minutes from the last time he spit up, mix room temperature water with a small amount of pure maple syrup, no more than a teaspoon. See how he does. If he throws up anymore, take him to Urgent Care if you can't get a hold of Brian. I'll ask your dad about Joshua. He leaves on a plane again in two days, and he needs to finish two landscaping jobs," Eula relayed.

"Okay, will do. I thought he let his landscaping business go after Larry passed? After all, he was his right-hand man and did much of the work. It's too much. He can't do it all. I gotta go, call me later. Thanks. Love you." Maria hung up.

"He only kept a few of the jobs because he's had them forever." Eula spoke into the dial tone. "Lord, let the water work for her. Oh, poo. I should have told her to add a smidge of ginger."

Eula texted her the information about the ginger root because she knew Maria kept all of that on hand. Then Eula turned her attention to making carrot juice. Her hands were getting tired from prepping the carrots and ginger, but she persisted, running the skinny orange logs through the juicer. It made the house smell delightful. After pouring the delicious liquid into the travel bottle and the glass jar, she started gathering the ingredients to make their smoothies for the next few days.

On the counter lay fresh spinach, cannellini beans, coconut yogurt, almond butter, Cacao powder, cinnamon, turmeric, almond milk, Hallelujah Acres Almost Chocolate protein powder, frozen blueberries, bananas and strawberries. She measured each ingredient into the blender with a touch of honey and liquefied for two to three minutes.

"Perfect," she said as she took a sample. The dryer buzzed for the third time in the background as Aaron scurried through the door to the bathroom. "Hi, hon. You okay?" she called after him.

"Yeah, just gotta go," he said.

She poured smoothies in a glass for each of them and used the rest to fill his travel bottles. Then she folded the clothes in the dryer and immediately hung Aaron's dress clothes since she didn't like ironing. She smiled at a well-accomplished morning.

Aaron came in and kissed her. "The house smells great; you juiced. Thanks for everything. You are the wind beneath my wings." He twirled her around.

"Your smoothie is on the counter. Did you have a good workout?" she asked.

"Yes, I definitely felt it. Smoothie is good. Did Maria call you? he questioned. "She tried to call me, but the phone was in the car."

"She wants me to pick up Joshua and bring him to her," Eula answered.

"Are you up for that? I can reschedule my job this afternoon and go with you," he responded.

"When will you do it? You leave on Sunday. No, it's okay."

"I want to be with you anyway." He went over next to her. "You know you want me to," he said in his playful voice.

"You're right. I do. Now I need to exercise before I forget it for the day, and then I will be sore on Monday because I haven't worked out in five days." She kissed him on the cheek. "Thanks."

"Lord, thank you for helping me accomplish those tasks. Please keep me safe as I work out," she prayed.

Aaron inserted the disc into the DVD player for her. Eula spread her hot pink mat on the floor and picked up her three-pound purple dumbbells. It felt good to get back into a routine after the rush of last week. She realized after traveling with Aaron for the last month that she liked being home; travelling was not something she wanted to do all the time. After completing the thirty-three-minute workout, she turned her attention to her back and knee stretches. Then she gathered her smoothie, Bible, journal, glasses, and water for her quiet time on the porch.

No sooner had she sat down, then her phone rang. "Shoot. I forgot to leave it in the house," she mused. "Hi, sweetie. How's the baby?" Eula asked.

"It worked! Hallelujah! He pooped a diaper full, now he is all giggly and happy. Thanks. Do you still want to get Joshua? If not, I understand. You and dad have a lot going on," Maria responded.

"Sure, what time should we pick him up? We'll spend the night and come home early in the morning." Eula winked at Aaron who walked outside and sat down in the chair.

He gave her a thumbs up sign. She then handed the phone to him so he could explain to his persistent daughter why he did not answer when she called. Eula laughed out loud. He took the phone and went back inside.

Chapter Seven
TENTACLES OF OBSESSION

Brian scrubbed and joined the others in the operating room. He was merely there as an observer, but the procedure remained the same. The tentacles of the lemon-sized tumor wove its way around the inner brain like an octopus wrapped tightly around its prey. It was aggressive. He had seen its kind many times before; radiation and chemotherapy did little to stop this monster's destruction. Unfortunately, as they cut away as much of the tumor as possible, being careful not to damage the delicate blood vessels in between, Brian could see another tumor growing behind it, impossible to reach without damaging the brain beyond repair. His heart sunk.

The surgeon's face reflected his horror. "Sew him up. There is nothing more we can do."

Brian would tell the grieving father today; it could not be prolonged. The boy had only a matter of days, and death was inevitable. Unless… He dialed the chief of oncology. "Sir, I know our experiment is in its trial stages, but in this case, what could it hurt? They would not be losing anything and could actually gain the boy's life. I know, but sir, please hear me out. I know it's not approved. It won't cost the hospital, nor the father anything. The grant will take care of it. No, I can't say I understand. Yes, sir. Thank you, anyway." The hospital was obsessed about following rules and saving money, even at the expense of their patients' lives, Brian thought. He held his head low as he hung up the phone. This was the third attempt and denial this week to let him try the island flower remedy. He went into the medicine room and sank to the floor. He did not know how much more of the politics he could take. He became a doctor to save, not to lose patient after patient to the Big C.

"Father, I don't understand why they won't let me try to help these people." Brian stood up and made his way to the waiting room. The boy's father sat against the wall. He lost his wife to cancer four years prior, and this was his oldest son. He ached for him, especially knowing he possibly had a cure that he wouldn't be able to try.

"Sir, follow me, please." Brian led him to his office. He thought of the Scripture in Job 13:28, "Man decays like a rotten thing, like a garment that is moth-eaten." "That is cancer," he said to himself.

"Unidentifiable," the caller ID said on Maria's home phone. She chose not to answer it. The call went to the voicemail. Joshua played happily on the floor with his toys. Eula and Aaron stepped out to get a bite to eat, taking Angel with them.

The baby monitor picked up the lullaby CD playing in the nursery. She opened the back door and let the cool air blow in, but the temptation to go out was too strong. She knelt down by him. "Hey, buddy, do you want to get your jacket and go on the porch with Mommy?"

He abruptly stood to his feet. He liked the outdoors as much as Maria. She put on his hat and jacket. The light on the phone flickered, but she did not want to answer it now. Brian always called her on the cell if he needed her, so she stuck it and the monitor in her pocket.

As she stood looking out at the aspen's silver dollar-shaped leaves swaying in the breeze, the wind felt like fairies dancing across her bare skin, like Daddy's butterfly kisses lighting softly on her cheek. This weather could wash all her worries away as she enjoyed her little boy playing sweetly at her feet.

Maria heard the garage door open. "Daddy must be home," she said excitedly as she scooped Joshua up in her arms. They ran to meet him as he came through the back door.

"Surprise!" they shouted.

Brian's downcast mouth turned upward as he reached for the boy and hugged him close. "Oh, how I needed to see you today. I love you both," he said as he leaned over to kiss Maria. "Where are your parents?"

"They went to get something to eat. I didn't feel like going out. Allon was sick again today, but no fever. I wish we could get his little intestines straightened out. Poor thing. The doctor just keeps saying, failure to thrive, but won't give me anything but formulas to try. I think the added "nutrition" or calories in them makes him constipated, then he gets so backed up it makes him throw up, but they won't listen to me," Maria shared.

Joshua wiggled out of his arms and headed to the patio door. "No, not now. It's getting dark. Tomorrow okay?" Maria said gently and switched on the safety latch.

"I know how that feels." Brian explained the denials to use his research. "Maybe we could try a little of the flower in a tea syrup, see what that does for Allon?"

"I don't know. He is super sensitive. Don't look discouraged. I trust you, but only if you will be home to monitor him. Let's wait until he has another episode though," Maria consoled.

Brian lit up. "Sounds good. It's different working on humans. Using mice is okay, but they don't respond the same to treatment. I know I could've helped that boy today. Now I'll never know. Is your mom picking up supper for me too?"

"Of course. Will you check the voicemail? I think we have a message? You know that thing is ancient, right? Of course, pretty soon there will be no such thing as a home phone; most people only use their cell now." She turned to Joshua. "You need a diaper change and a bath." She scurried him off to the bathroom.

Brian walked over to the machine. A deep, familiar voice echoed through the machine, "Hello, my friends. You will be receiving a package from me soon. Please, trust me, and do as instructed. Your friend."

"Not now," he said through clenched teeth. "Daddy, please. It had been a little less than two years since Larry and Adaline passed. They only had a few more months with Joshua, and he barely had any remaining time off at work. "God, what am I going to do? Maria can't take this right now. She won't be able to handle the twins and temporary custody of Joshua alone. Breathe, Brian. Breathe. Wait, it's about Angel. It can't be time already. She is too young to be heir to a throne. What if, they couldn't rescue her dad? Don't go there, Brian. Calm down. Get it together."

About then the doorbell rang, Maria's parents were back. Angel came busting through the door. "Daddy, Daddy!" She threw herself up into his arms.

"Brian, are you okay? You look like you saw a ghost?" Aaron questioned.

"Yeah, hard day at work. We are seeing more and more children diagnosed with brain cancer, and the board is unwilling to try any alternative methods, even with proof that they work," Brian answered. "Excuse me, I need to go change. Maria is bathing Joshua. Angel, Daddy will be out in a minute. Go to your room, and finish your homework, please. I'll read with you in a bit." He kissed her on the head.

Eula looked at Aaron. She placed their food bags on the kitchen counter. "I think they should go out after the kids go to bed for coffee and some time together."

"Yeah, and we'll go to bed early," he teased.

Brian waited eagerly for the Fed-Ex package. Maria slept in after a rough night up with the twins. Angel was at school and Joshua back at his grandparents. He was doing better about leaving them. The altercations with Beatrice always made it difficult. However, she seemed better at times. Frederick had made noticeable changes in the way he handled himself and seemed to move more in humility. He handled the child with loving care, and Joshua always ran to him first. Aaron and Eula left the previous day to go home after a nice visit. The children loved it when they were there, and Brian wished they lived closer.

He could see the blue and white truck coming down their street. He grabbed a jacket and stood at the end of the driveway.

"Must be important for you to be standing out in this drizzle?" The Fed-Ex worker commented.

"Yes, it is. Thank you," Brian said as he signed the portable pad.

He tore open the envelope and went to his car to read its contents. There in Rojomen's hand writing was explicit details, money, and tickets to bring Angel to an unknown location. It would be revealed step by step, and they would have guides at each point. As usual, there was no return address. They had two weeks before their journey would begin. He breathed in deeply, "So it begins, Lord. We promised. Please give me the strength to do what you have asked us to do. Help Maria."

Brian sat on the bed next to Maria and gently shook her. There would be no good time to break this news; now was the time. "Honey, wake up. We need to talk," he held the papers in his hand.

"Are the babies awake? Fifteen more minutes." She turned over.

"No, now sweetie," Brian said.

She sat up and rubbed her eyes. "What's that?" She pointed to the envelope in his hands.

He looked at her compassionately and handed her the papers. "It's different than he told us when he brought her to us. Something has changed. Maybe it's a good thing?" Brian raised his eyebrows.

"No, Brian. Not now. I'm not ready for this. We can't lose her too. It's not fair." She threw the papers on the bed and rolled over on her side.

He snuggled in next to her. "We promised. Remember what you said when we got the twins. Somehow deep inside you knew. Maybe Jesus was preparing us, and we didn't know it. She'll always be ours. We don't know if they are going to keep her. Why didn't he do what he said? This is all different. Remember, when he brought her to us that first day? He said they would take her, and we would never see her again. Her memory of us would be wiped away. Why would he ask me to bring her and tell me to trust him?" He pulled her over to look into her eyes. "We have to trust that Jesus is working this out for good, no matter how hard it is."

"I know. What about work?" Maria asked.

"I'm going to ask for family leave. Rojomen sent enough to cover any expenses we might have, including time off. I'll tell Angel that she is going on a medical adventure with me. You know how she likes to play doctor. She doesn't have a good grip on time yet. What about your parents and Barbie?" Brian inquired.

"My parents have been very busy. I'll tell them you are taking her on a research trip. They won't question it. Please pray. I need to call Alesha and tell her I may need her double time when you leave. Barbie is busy with Ken, and it seems pretty serious. They were looking at rings the other day. Did you know he can manage her care concerning the Lyme's disease because he is a doctor at the Mayo Clinic where she had treatment? Pretty cool, if you ask me. That also means if she is doing too much, he will pull back the reigns so it doesn't affect her health. I'm scared though. The court date for Joshua comes up soon.

I don't know if I could handle losing both of them at the same time," Maria replied.

"Let's call Pastor Stroke and ask for prayer. We don't need to mention specifics, except in Joshua's case. Maybe you can pull out the study you did with him when you were going through counseling to help you prepare. I'll see if I can ask for family leave starting next week for an indefinite time. That way we can take Angel by to see everyone important in her life and you can have some down time before we leave and spend time one-on-one with her. I'll call her school and let them know she's going on a trip with me. Her teacher will like the idea." He pulled her close. "I love you more than all the stars in the sky and fish in the sea."

Chapter Eight
MYSTERY UNFOLDS

Maria sat looking out the airport window, holding Angel in her lap. "Please, Daddy, bring her back to me," she silently prayed. The twins in the stroller slept peacefully. The intercom above called passengers to their final boarding calls.

Angel jumped down and looked up into her mama's eyes. "Why do you look sad? Daddy and I'll be home soon."

"I know, honey, but Mommy will miss you very much! You are a smart girl. Daddy can use your help. You are going to make a good doctor someday, my little princess." Maria flashed back to the party they had when they announced Angel to the world and the blanket she wrapped the infant in to soothe her. A tear trickled down her cheek.

Angel reached up and wiped it away. "I love you more than all the lollipops in the world." She threw her arms open wide. They had been playing the "I love you more" game since her toddler stage.

Maria grabbed her and whispered in her ear. "I love you more than all the sugar in all the lollipops in the world."

Angel cackled with glee. Brian came back from the ticket counter. "Our first stop is Chicago. I'll call you when we land there and give you our next destination. I have copies of her adoption papers and immunization, plus both our passports. Everything will be okay. As long as we have cell towers, I'll call or text you, but be prepared. When we get to the remote areas, you may not hear from us for a couple weeks. I don't know how long this will take. If the court calls, see if you can stall. I love you more than words can say. Pray as much as you can. We need to go through security now." He kissed the twins gently on the head. "Cling to Jesus and these babies. They'll keep you sane. Do whatever you need to, to be okay. Promise?" Brian held her close.

"I promise. I feel like I can't breathe." Maria tried to give words to her pain.

"Yes, you can. Don't believe a lie. As Abraham told his men when he took Isaac, look in my eyes; we will return,'" Brian said with all the confidence surging within him. He had to be strong for her.

Maria gave him one last hug and a longing kiss. She bent down and hugged Angel with all her might, not wanting to let her go. Then she watched as they made their way through security. The little girl wore a pink dress with lace around the middle and white bobby socks. Her hair braided with a variety of plastic bows, the way she liked it.

Maria memorized every detail of her thin frame. She was getting much taller and had grown several inches in the last year. Her height was way above the fiftieth percentile, and her weight was just under the thirtieth percentile, according to the growth chart. Truly a princess, beautiful inside and out, the special creation of a loving God. She would make an excellent leader with her compassionate and intuitive heart.

Abbie started crying and brought Maria back to the moment. She made her way to the nursing area inside the public bathroom. The couches were comfortable but not very private. Her heart was breaking, but she made the best effort to do as Brian asked and put her attention on the twins. She fed both and headed toward home. The rain outside matched the way she felt on the inside.

After bathing the twins, she cried herself to sleep watching a *Soaking Psalms* DVD. The phone rang a little after 10:00 p.m. Brian and Angel made it in to the O'Hare International Airport.

"Hey, babe. Sorry to wake you. I wanted to let you know we made it to the hotel. It looks like we'll be flying to South Hampton, England tomorrow. Angel is asleep, but I'll give her a kiss for you. She did amazing on the flight. A little girl next to us kept crying and our sweet one would lean as far as she could over to her, share her doll and make funny animal noises to make her laugh. I'm beat. I'll call you before we board tomorrow. Love you." Brian blew a kiss into the phone.

"Love you too." Maria poured herself a hot cup of tea. There was not any point in going back to sleep, at least one of the twins would be waking up to be fed soon. She picked up her Bible and slipped into her recliner. It fell open to Psalms 65:11, "You crown the year with your goodness and your paths drip with abundance."

"Glory to God. We receive that Jesus. Fill my heart with your peace and assurance." She knelt by her chair. "Daddy, I give back to you the gift you gave me. Thank you for the years we had. No matter how difficult it gets, please help me to trust you," she prayed.

The TV turned on and about scared her out of her wits. Then she realized Brian had a favorite show he recorded, and he preset the TV and DVD to turn on and record. She was sure he did not mean for the volume to be turned up. Joshua played with the remote. He loved to turn it on and off, laughing hysterically each time. Evidently, she had forgotten to hide it the last time he visited.

She settled back into her spot and continued her search in the Scriptures for more encouraging promises. Psalms burst forth like a desert in the spring. Even though David laments his situations, he always turns back to the one he lives for and ends in praise to his maker. If we take the time to look between the hidden crevices and dark places of life, we can find beauty hidden there, compared to pearl within the oyster shell.

Her moments of solitude came to a halt as Abbie started to cry. Maria prepared two bottles and brought Abbie into the living room with her. "Listen, my sweet girl. That is the sound of peace. Jesus met me here tonight. I so need Him." She burped her and played a few minutes, then rocked her to sleep. After laying her in the pink polka dotted crib, Angel picked out, Maria put her fingers to her lips, kissed and touched the side of Abbie's head and the crib. Then she gently picked up Allon and took him to her rocker. She whispered in his ear the same thing she told his sister and tickled his feet to wake him up. He got red-faced and angry, but she did not care because he needed to eat.

She kissed his face tenderly, wiped it with a wet cloth, and placed the bottle to his lips. Her arm fell asleep, but she waited patiently. He fell asleep three times, but she got four ounces down him, and burped him. "Good job, my Snuckems," she said. "Mommy loves you, and we'll do whatever we need to for you to be happy and healthy. The tea daddy made you is working. Two bottles down with no spitting up. Hallelujah!"

She wanted to keep an eye on him; therefore, she placed him in the swing. A red envelope on the table caught her attention. "Hmmm, I didn't see that earlier." It was a letter from Uncle Ron. He and his fiancée were in Medicine Park, Oklahoma looking for a home. She had a job offer there, and he could work from anywhere because he worked remotely and traveled a lot. He said he had run into some old friends of the family and wanted to see if Brian remembered, Craig and Kathy. They were building homes and cabins in Medicine Park. He said they were doing well and planned to marry before they settled on where to live. It would not be too big a to-do, as they both had been married previously. They would make it good in the sight of God and get things started on the right foot. He ended his usual way, signed with love, gave kisses to the young'uns, Uncle Ron. P.S. Will call soon.

Maria laughed at his antics because he never got around to calling. She headed back to bed and dreamed of holding her little Angel. Her night was filled with pleasant memories from the first time she looked into her big, dark eyes, up until the night before they left when she read her a story and tucked her into bed with their ritual, wrapping the covers tightly around her and saying, "Snug as a bug in a rug."

Brian called the next morning to say he loved her and they were leaving to catch the shuttle. Angel chatted with her all the way to the terminal. It was like the birds Maria fed at the park. Chirping, chirping, chirping non-stop. She giggled listening to her. The excitement in her voice was contagious. She described every detail of the flight, even how her belly got a little queasy from the sudden lift in the air.

"Do you know what it is called?" Maria asked.

"I think Daddy said it was turbulence." Angel responded, not missing a beat. "I got to go now. I miss you. I love you."

"Very good. I love you to the moon and back. Give Daddy a kiss for me," Maria responded.

Brian got on the phone. "It looks like we fly from South Hampton to Pointe Noire Airport in the Republic of Congo. It'll be a long flight with no time in between. I love you. Don't worry. We'll be okay."

"Okay honey, I love you more than all this world has to offer. Come back to me," Maria spoke softly.

Chapter Nine
FEARFUL HAPPENINGS

Brian carried Angel to the private jet stationed outside the landing strip. It had been a grueling sixteen hours since they left South Hampton, and his legs ached from cramped flying conditions and sitting too long. They had switched planes at least three times. He laid her in the seat next to him and then stretched his legs out as far as they would go, moved them back and forth, then rubbed arnica cream up and down the sides of his calves.

"When will we get to the airport near the sight of our convoy deploy?" he asked his guide.

He spoke fluent English. "I'm not at liberty to tell you that yet. Try to rest. You've a long journey ahead."

Brian did not understand the secrecy. It was evident they were going into the Republic of Congo, and it could be dangerous. There were two guards stationed at each end of the small plane. His mind could not process anymore, and he fell asleep to the rumble of the motor. It felt like he was awakened within minutes, but it was actually hours.

Angel pulled on his sleeve. "Daddy, I got to go to the potty. Where are we?"

Brian sat up. "Look, there is a bathroom." He took her hand and led her to the door. "You go. I'll stand right here." He pointed to a spot directly outside the door.

"Okay, I'm hungry," she whimpered. "I miss Mommy."

"I know. It's okay. Use the potty, and then we'll eat." He knelt down and hugged her. "I know. Go on in now," he directed.

After she finished, he picked her up and held her until they got to their seats. "Look. I brought your favorite." He pulled out an almond butter and jelly sandwich, fruit cup, and chips. He wiped her hands, prayed, and handed the food to her. She was not at all happy.

Brian knew she was tired, but they still had a long way to go. He told her a story of a princess in a faraway land who needed to get back to her people. "They needed her to teach them all the things she learned from her travels, like how to grow food and irrigate plants."

Angel cocked her eyebrow up like Brian did when he was thinking.

"Irrigate means run water to plants, like your mama's rose bushes and flower garden. The princess also had special medicine to heal the sick people."

A big smile spread across her face. "I'm the princess, huh?" she asked.

"Well, of course you are. On this trip will you try to be the strong, brave, and helpful princess I know you are? I need your help," Brian said.

"Yes, daddy." She threw her arms around his neck.

"Sir, we are about to land. I need to ask you to put these bags over your heads. You don't have to be scared. It is a precautionary measure. Even I'll be wearing one. Rojomen has given you the best guards in the country. He won't let you down. Once we get past the convoy sight, they will remove them. It'll take about an hour though," the guard explained.

"Angel, do you understand. We are playing a game like hide-n-seek, except instead of closing our eyes, we'll wear these. Okay? Daddy will hold your hand the entire time. I will not leave you." Brian placed the knapsack bag over her head and then his. "Oh God, please keep us safe."

They were escorted off the plane into jeeps. Brian could tell by the sound of the engines and the rough ride that they were on dirt roads. He had worked a medical clinic on the reservation back home during his rotations in medical school. Those roads would knock your spine out of alignment. He pulled Angel over into his lap and wrapped his arms around her. It seemed like they drove for more than an hour. The air seemed thick with humidity. He thought he might have a panic attack if they did not stop soon. He kept breathing in and out slowly.

"Daddy, I'm scared," Angel expressed.

"It's okay to be a little afraid. It helps us remember Jesus is always with us. Close your eyes, and pretend you are looking up at the stars, like when you and I are camping in our backyard. Can you see the galaxy? There's the big and little dipper." He encouraged her to use her imagination station, and she began to name off the stars he had taught her.

It was not long before she fell asleep in his arms.

"We're almost at base camp. We'll stay there for the night and begin our journey to the Woodlands tomorrow." The guard spoke in hushed tones.

The jeeps stopped and someone pulled the bags off their heads. "Welcome. Welcome," he said as he shook Brian's hand. He took Angel from Brian's arms and said, "Come, follow me." The man went into a large tent. He tenderly laid the sleeping child on a cot.

Brian looked outside the flap of the door, campfires were spread throughout, and armed men sat around them. "Soldiers?" he asked.

"Yes, the best. I am Rojomen's brother. He has left me in charge to bring you and the princess safely to him!" he exclaimed as if he had won a prize.

"I see, brother?" Brian knew the story of what happened to Rojomen's family.

"Let me explain. I'm his brother because our master rescued both of us, and we grew up together. Rest. There is water here for washing and here for drinking." He pointed to a basin and a jug. "You must only drink water from the jugs, or you will get very sick."

Brian pulled up the empty cot next to Angel's and quickly fell asleep. His body exhausted.

They were deep into the woods now. The convoy left them to travel on foot. Angel was handling it like a real trooper. She attached quickly to Rojomen's brother, and he became her guardian. He could silence her quicker than Brian ever could with his firm but gentle tone.

"There is a camp up ahead. We'll lodge there for the night. We've a covenant with this tribe so we can trade and borrow with them. It'll be safe," the guard explained.

As they approached the outer edges of the tribal boundary, Brian could hear wailing. "This doesn't sound good. He picked up Angel and placed her on his shoulders. Be quiet."

"Stay here," The guardian ordered the troop. "I'll find out what's happening." He returned within minutes. "There is death in the camp. Do you have medicine?" he questioned, eyes wide with terror.

Brian had never seen such intense boils in his life. He could not imagine how Rojomen directed his men through this area knowing Angel accompanied them. The anger rose up within him, but quickly extinguished when he saw the number of children and the pain of the people. He gave his daughter strict orders not to come out of the sterilized tent the men had erected upon first entering the village. He told the guard, "If I'm to help these people, you and your men must do exactly as I say."

His heart melted as a tiny infant was placed in his hands. He worked for hours trying to relieve her fever and pain. The guard assured him that Rojomen told the soldiers to protect Brian and Angel at all costs. But how was he to believe this was part of the plan?

"I'm a doctor, not a miracle worker," he mumbled under his breath.

A still small voice spoke to his heart, "But you know the miracle worker; he lives inside of you and works through your hands. He put the desire in you to be a doctor, maybe even for such a time as this."

Brian sent the people away. He needed to check on Angel and take a break. The words echoed in his mind. As he entered the first barrier curtain of their tent, he took off the protective clothing and gloves and washed his hands and arms before stepping into their sleeping quarters. The six-year-old, tall, lean, and extremely intelligent little girl held her doll with great compassion as she took its temperature and listened to its heartbeat.

Every day she told Brian, "Daddy, I want to help people, just like you."

Brian insisted the men and women helping wear gloves and masks. Three separate huts were erected for the different levels of the infection. He prayed for more time as death enveloped the camp. Fires were continually lit to keep out the wild animals. Steaming metal pots were set up at each station for body cleansing. He scoured himself before going into the tents and refused to let Angel touch him. At first, she cried, but he explained the best he could, and she understood.

She heard Brian tell the story of the miracle flower from Neatorama many times. One evening before bed she asked, "Daddy, what about the flower? Can't you use it?"

"Oh, sweetie, I'm not sure if they have it here. It's an island flower. Even if they do, it would take too many days to find it. He was exhausted.

"But Jesus will help us. I'll pray." She bowed her head.

Brian's mind flashed to Maria, Joshua, and the twins at home. Her heart had been broken when Rojomen summoned them, but it brought them hope that Brian was asked to escort her. Nonetheless, she cried for days. She continued to tell Angel stories of a young princess who must go on a great adventure, find a cure for her people, and return to her true home. At the time, as Brian watched her brush the child's hair, he had no clue how true the story would become.

"Amen! Daddy, I said, Amen!" Angel called to him.

"Amen! I'm sorry. I was thinking about Mommy and your brothers."

"Don't forge Abbie. I miss them too," her lip started to quiver.

He wanted nothing more than to gather her into his arms, but he would not dare take the risk.

"Doctor! Doctor!" a frightened voice yelled. "Come at once!"

"Daddy, please don't go." Angel started to cry.

"Honey, it's okay. You know there are really sick children out there. Daddy must go help them." He formed his arms into a hug and blew her a kiss.

"Yes, Daddy, you must go." She hugged him back from the air between them.

He called the lady caregiver back into the tent. After she scrubbed and changed, Brian told her through the translator, "Please hold her and pray. She knows how. She's very good at it." He winked at Angel.

He lost the infant and an adult female that evening. This camp had burned the bodies of ten of its members since the awful plagued began. Brian collapsed and cried out in desperation, "Help me, Jesus."

Chapter Ten
CARING HEARTS

Maria looked at the man on the corner with frazzled threads on his gloves, the tips of his fingers sticking out, and holes in his shoes. A cold front had moved in, catching everyone off guard. It was unseasonably cold for this time of year; it was freezing outside. Even though his sign said, "Need work. Hungry," she thought, he needs something now.

The twins were sleeping peacefully and Joshua was looking at his dinosaur book, making grunts here and there. Maria thought about Brian and Angel, but could not linger there too long or she would lose control. "Were they hot, cold, hungry, or...? No!" she said. "They are fine."

A horn honked behind her, and she was perplexed about what to do. She rolled down the window and yelled to the man, "Stay here! I'll be back soon!"

As Maria waited in the drive thru at McDonalds, she tapped into her curbside pickup at Walmart and ordered shoes, a toboggan, gloves, canned tuna, hygiene items, and other non-perishable foods.

"Oops, I almost forgot a jacket," she said out loud.

"For who mommy?" Joshua asked.

"The man at the light. He needs a little help, and we don't want him to catch a cold. Remember Jesus tells us to help others if we can," Maria replied.

Joshua was the most compassionate little boy she had ever known. His eyes sparkled with excitement.

"Can I help?" he said gleefully.

"Yes, you may," she responded.

Maria placed her food order and drove through. She told Joshua when she rolled down the window to hand the gentleman the food and say, "Jesus loves you." He did exactly as he was instructed. Then she motioned for the man to come to her window. There was a tear in his eyes.

"I'll be back. If you could meet me over at the gas station, I'll have some more things for you," Maria told him.

"Thank you, Ma'am. God bless you," he replied and walked over to the curb, laid down his sign, bowed his head, and then ate.

"Look, Mommy; he is praying." Joshua clapped his hands and one of the babies started to cry. "Oops."

"It's okay, honey. We've got to feed them soon anyway." She said a grateful prayer of thanks that no one was driving up behind her, and then she pulled into a secluded spot in the Walmart parking lot. She handed Joshua his fries and unlatched Abbie to feed her. Baby Allon slept soundly. He was the smaller of the two. It felt like he would sleep through every feeding, if Maria didn't wake him.

Joshua was due to meet his grandparents before 5:00 p.m., which made Maria anxious. Fortunately, this baby ate quickly and burped well. She drove over to the curbside pickup area, but the attendant was nowhere in sight.

"I don't have time for this." She loaded them into a buggy, strapping the smallest to her chest, found the manager, and asked for her groceries to be delivered outside and loaded into her car. He apologized profusely.

By the time she made it to the Circle K, it was a quarter past 4 pm. "Where is he?" she snorted.

"Mommy, look!" Joshua pointed toward the lamppost at the far end of the lot. He was leaning up against it, reading. She honked the horn and waved.

The sixtyish year old, scruffy-bearded, rosy-cheeked man smiled and waltzed over to the car.

"What are you reading?" Maria asked as she opened her door.

"My Bible, I know it's worn like me, but I read it every day. These darn glasses make it difficult though," he said.

"I got you some stuff to keep you warm," Maria replied.

"You didn't have to do that, but thank you kindly. I try to make it to the shelter every evening, but sometimes they are already full," he responded.

Maria hesitated, "May I ask you a question?"

He nodded yes.

She continued, "Why are you out here? Don't you have family? Somewhere you could go?"

"I have a step-daughter, but she kicked me out after my wife died. It wasn't her fault. After Martha died, I just gave up. I started drinking, and you know." He held his head in shame.

Allon started crying from his car seat. Maria glared at her watch. "Oh, my gosh! I gotta go. I'll be back another time. Here's my card. Any night you don't get into the shelter, call me. I'll see what I can do."

"Thank you!" he expressed as they pulled away.

Joshua waved bye. Maria buckled her seat belt and silently prayed. "Lord, I can't be late again. Please, have mercy."

Beatrice sat with her arms folded. "She's late again. Ridiculous, if you ask me."

"Now remember, hon, we are trying to be a little more understanding. We promised to work on what's best for Joshua. Adaline would want us too." He patted her on the arm, and she did not flinch away.

She knew he was right, but this whole mess had turned their lives upside down. She had always been in control, a take charge woman, and now, well, let's just say, everything was out of control. Look at her; not even her nails had been done in weeks. Keeping after a toddler, playing with and tending to his needs above her own, she did not know if she was cut out for this. Frederick desperately wanted the boy, so she had no choice but to fight for him. She had won, or had she?

The baby screamed blood curdling cries from his car seat. Maria could not take it. She pulled the car over to the shoulder, texted Frederick, and took the infant from his carrier. "Okay, honey, Mommy is sorry."

She rocked him back and forth, pulled the bottle from her cooler, shook it well, and placed it in his pursed lips. More than anything, she wanted to bond with these babies. He slowly sipped, and after four ounces, she burped him. Abbie was eating well over eight ounces now. Maria prayed he would be soon too.

"Thank God it stayed down," she muttered.

Joshua and Abbie fell asleep. Maria buckled Allon in his seat and pushed the soothing CD into the player. Her mom knew exactly what she needed during these turbulent times and sent her the music a few days before. It calmed her nerves. "No hurries, no worries," she repeated to herself as she put the car in gear. This was not a non-caring, irresponsible response; it just helped her stay peaceful when things were out of her control, which was most of the time lately.

"Thank you, Jesus, for reminding me what is truly important," she whispered.

Beatrice stood with her hands on her hips, but Frederick came over to the minivan to help her.

"I don't know how you do it," he said sympathetically.

"I love them all and pray a lot. I ask forgiveness when I'm late and do what I can, the best I can. I'm really sorry. May we sit down inside for a minute, please," she said weakly.

She explained what happened. "Beatrice, I don't want you to think I don't care that I'm late, I do. I'm sorry," Maria apologized.

"Let me get this straight. You helped a homeless man, opened your car door to a complete stranger with my grandson in the vehicle?" Beatrice lashed out.

Red slowly creeped up her neck to her ears and into Maria's cheeks.

"He was an old man. It was good for Joshua to see us helping someone else, to have compassion. Don't you want him to care about others?" Maria argued.

"That's absurd! Of course, I do!" Beatrice took the sleeping child from Maria's arms abruptly.

He started to cry. "Please, not this way again," Maria begged. "You promised."

She stormed off to the car with Joshua kicking and screaming for Maria.

Frederick apologized, "I'm sorry. She is trying. It will get better. I'm working on her. Hang in there." He patted Maria's shoulder.

She sat in the restaurant booth and cried. "Is there nothing I can do about these encounters with Beatrice? Lord, help me. Father, she didn't let me kiss him bye. Please keep them safe, and let him know I love him," she prayed.

She would call later to check on him. Oh, how she missed Brian. Beatrice was much kinder when he was around.

Maria dialed her mom's number and left a message, "Mom, I know you and Dad are out of town, but I can't get ahold of Barbie, and I need to talk. Please call me when you get a chance."

Then she called Alesha to see if she could help with the twins. She was exhausted and needed rest. The young woman did not answer, so

Maria left another voicemail. The windmill coffee sign caught her eye. She pulled in and ordered a warm chai.

"Nothing like a warm drink on a day like this," the barista said cheerfully.

"You are right. Thank you." The liquid soothed her.

The drive to the house was a little icy, but Maria eased up the driveway slowly. Both babies were crying now. She began to sing the lullaby she had often sung to Angel to comfort her. Behind her she heard the toot of a car horn and looked to see Alesha bounding up the driveway. The tall, thin twenty-one-year-old had not only become her babysitter, but a trusted friend.

"Sorry, I was at work. Couldn't answer my phone," She said.

"Thank God you are here. Thanks for coming; it has been a day," Maria responded.

Alesha went to the other side of the van and pulled Allon out, cradling him safely in her arms. "Shhh. Shhh, now, it's okay; Auntie Alesha is here."

"You are a lifesaver. God knew I needed you." Maria put her arm around the girl. They took the babies inside, fed, changed, and played with them. Then she demanded Maria take a hot bath and nap. She delightfully obeyed the young woman's commands.

Chapter Eleven
HEZEKIAH'S CURE

Brian held the small, lifeless body in his hands, the fourth child to die in two days. It was more than he could bear. He had sent Angel on with the warriors from Rojomen's tribe, one of the hardest things he had ever done. He had no choice but to trust them with his daughter's life. No longer could he risk her being in the camp. It was too dangerous.

His mind still pictured her face, and his heart could hear her voice pleading, "No, Daddy, I want to stay with you."

"Father God, I don't know how to help these people; the young and old are dying. If you don't do something quick, this village will be lost. These people will die without you. Help me, please." Brian cupped his head in his hands.

Out of nowhere, like a piece of paper blowing in the wind, a Scripture in II Kings 20:7 enlightened Brian's mind. It tells the story of King Hezekiah on his death bed; the prophet Isaiah is told to take a lump of figs and place it on the king's boil, and the king recovers.

"That's it!" Brian danced around the camp yelling, "Praise the Lord! Thank you, Jesus!"

The men eyed him eerily. They thought he was delirious from a lack of sleep.

Rojomen's brother left four warriors with Brian to escort him safely out when the time came, one spoke English. He questioned, "What is it?"

"Figs, do you have figs?" Brian asked.

The man translated his question to one of the tribal men.

"Day's journey," he said.

"You must go immediately. Harvest as many as you can carry, quickly now. Go! Godspeed." Brian demanded.

Wailing came from the tent at the far end of the camp. It pierced the darkness like the coyotes on rampage for food in the Arizona wilderness. Brian's skin crawled. If he never made it out of here, at least Angel was safe and would see her father. He accomplished that much. "Shake it off," he told himself. "Sorry, Father, I trust you."

He picked up his bag and walked toward the luminous night. The chief knelt by a woman holding a child. This was not common for a leader of a tribe. Watching his people die one by one, now his son, brought him to his knees. No one but Brian was allowed to enter. He gently took the child from the mother's arms. There were still faint breaths.

"He's not dead." Brian wrapped the child in a blanket and carried him to the medical tent. The parents did not follow. The tribe council had quarantined everyone to their tents. They could not risk losing their chief.

Brian worked endlessly into the morning hours trying to bring the boy's fever down. He was in a coma, his body's way of resting and fighting. Every hour or so a man came and gave word to his parents that the child was still alive. The seven-year-old boy was strong despite the sickness that consumed him. He was a fighter. The dehydration from the fever was the hardest to treat with their limited medical supplies and being miles away from any source of help. The Holy Spirit directed Brian to coconut water as a source of electrolytes.

The boy's fever broke around mid-morning. He came to, shaking violently. Brian administered seizure medication.

"Not a good sign," Brian translated.

The boy woke up enough to take small sips of the milky white liquid about an hour later. Unlike the other victims, he had not broken out with boils.

"What was different? Was he looking at a different strain of bacteria all together?" he questioned himself. He told the translator, "I must talk to the parents."

After another hour of deliberation through the translator, Brian realized there may be no answer other than his desperate cries to the Father. The next morning victory cries echoed through the camp as the search party marched in, carrying heavy poles laden with figs.

Brian's mind flashed to a picture of Joshua and Caleb's men in the Bible when taking samples of the bounty from the Promised Land.

He started spouting off orders and went full throttle. They carried the figs to Brian's tent. He again read the scripture about the figs, paying careful attention not to miss anything, and he prayed for direction. He instructed the men to boil water over the fires throughout the camp and to keep them going throughout the night. By dawn, Brian made a thick fig paste and sterilized every piece of equipment they would need to administer the thick anointment.

One by one, starting with the sickest children and the elderly, he applied the last of his antibiotic cream and the fig remedy on each boil. He prayed over each patient, gave strict instructions to the families to drink the coconut juice every hour, not to touch any boil site, and to cleanse their dwellings, or tear them down all together.

Brian gave the chief's son coconut water every fifteen minutes through a rendition of a straw he carved from the skin of the miombo tree. The boy began to improve and was able to sit up.

After seeing improvements among the tribe, Brian decided he must check on his daughter and make sure she was safe. He would need to leave these people in God's hands. He gathered the translator, the chief, and able-bodied people around the campfire.

"You asked me when I came, 'Why do you stay?' Now, I must tell you before I go." Brian explained the gospel and love of Jesus to them. He led them in a prayer. They all accepted this Jesus who came into their camp and healed their tribe through his servant. He wept with them. Never before had their chief seen such a humble man.

The chief took off the beaded chain from around his neck and placed it around Brian. He placed his head on Brian's forehead, a sign of honor and thankfulness. "Thank you, my brother," he said.

The ladies prepared satchels of flatbread for Brian and his men. He left the medical tent and all the supplies. He asked them to burn the other two tents. He carried only the essentials.

He and the four men appointed to watch over and lead him headed out as the rays of the sun hit the forest canopy. They walked through the sauna-like jungle, the heat and humidity almost unbearable. At times, Brian felt as if he was being smothered. Their long sleeves protected them from the massive biting insects. He recognized the mosquitos, but the other ones gave him the creeps.

He shuddered as he called to the leader, "How much farther?"

"We'll camp over that ridge. It's not safe to go on in the dark of night."

Brian wanted to argue, but he knew better. His exhausted body begged to differ with his mind that wanted to press on because of his daughter. In the distance he could hear the noise of men shouting in vicious tones. His party ducked down behind some brush and pulled him low, covering his mouth and sending quiet signs throughout. He prayed silently, "Calm my fears. Father, keep us safe. Get me to Angel."

The warrior party passed within a few hundred feet. They sat deathly still, daring not to breathe. He thought he was going to pass out. Once the men could no longer be heard in the distance, they continued to move quietly toward their destination. A couple of the men scouted ahead to find a cave within the mountain wall.

Brian never felt darkness like he did that night. He could not see his hand in front of him as he lay on the cave's unbelievably cold, hard surface. He dreamed of Maria and his children. Then flood waves of emotion overcame him as he relived the terror of the Neatorama island. The massive beast lunged toward him with elongated teeth and sharp claws.

The translator pulled hard on Brian's sleeve. "Wake up, Doctor. You are having a nightmare. Wake up." He threw water on his face.

Brian jumped up in fighting stance. He was sweating profusely. The translator handed him a cup of water. "You okay?" he asked. "We leave in five minutes."

He longed to wrap his arms around his wife. He could not imagine how hard this was on her, not knowing. Brian wrote in his journal when they stopped for a break, "Not knowing is sometimes the hardest thing God asks us to do. When Abraham ventured out in faith, he did not know where he was going. He left the people he loved, trusted, and obeyed. Help my wife, and me to trust you, Lord."

Barbie and Ken left the restaurant at a little after seven. She thought he would drop her at home, but instead he headed east on the 202 freeway. It was dark out, and she was curious what he was up to, but she held her peace for the moment. They drove in silence, his hand clasped around hers.

He turned on the exit to the zoo. Her curiosity got the better of her.

"What are you up too?" she prodded.

"For me to know, and you to find out. If I told you, it wouldn't be a surprise, now would it?" He pulled into a parking space at Papago Park.

"We can't hike in the dark, you fanatic," she joked.

"Wanna bet?" He pulled flashlights and a small cooler from under his seat.

"I'm game," she said, pulling her hoodie on.

They walked up the winding path leading to the back of the red rock with the hole in it, and after ten minutes they stood in its opening.

"The scenery from up here is gorgeous. I've never seen it at night before. I'm pretty sure we aren't supposed to be here after dark." She cocked her eyebrows.

"Yes, it is. Gorgeous, I mean." He pulled her into his embrace and kissed her.

Then he threw a blanket on the rock and held her hand to lower her down. He knelt beside her and opened the cooler, bringing out two small filled wine glasses and dark chocolate covered strawberries.

"You really know how to impress a lady. Where did you get all this romanticism from?" she joked.

"My dad. He was as cool as a cucumber." He put a strawberry to her lips.

He sat down and faced her. "More?" he asked. She shook her head yes.

He put a strawberry in his mouth and placed it up to her. They met in the middle, and she felt something cool and hard on his tongue. His slid it onto hers. "Be careful now. Don't swallow."

She lowered her mouth and allowed the object to fall in his outstretched hand. He took a cloth and wiped it clean. Then he held her hand in his, looked up into her startled eyes and said, "Barbie, I love you. Will you marry me?"

"Yes! Yes! I'd be crazy not to!" She slid the ring onto her finger, fell into his arms, and kissed him passionately.

Brian woke to the crackling of a fire and felt its radiant warmth spread over his entire body. One of the men held a stick over the open flame, the small lizard-looking creature sizzled and popped. It made his stomach queasy, but his stomach gurgled for something to fill it.

The man handed Brian the stick. "Eat. Long journey today. You need your strength." he commanded.

Not wanting to offend them, Brian did as he was told, but the meat did not settle well or stay down. Try as he might to talk himself out of being sick, it did not work. He rushed out of the cave. The men laughed. He did not see what was funny.

"You've never had lizard before?" the man questioned.

"No, not that I know of," Brian gruffly answered.

Up to this point the men were serious. He was glad they could get a good laugh at his expense.

They traversed through the thick forest for what seemed like an eternity. Brian's legs ached, and he could hardly breathe. He could see a mountain in the distance. The translator spoke, "Rojomen has given specific instructions for us to take the hidden passageway beneath the mountain. We must make absolutely certain that there are no intruders following us. This is the most difficult and dangerous part of our journey. Are you ready?"

He could only think of the responsibility Maria would have in raising the twins if something happened to him, how her heart had already been devastated at losing Joshua and Angel. A rustle in the thicket brought his mind back to the present. "Yes, I'm ready. I will do whatever I need to do to see my daughter again."

The mountain stood out like the Great Wall of China, but as quickly as they had turned to climb the mountainous path, they ducked behind a water fall hidden beneath the thick forest covering. They followed the narrow path between the rocks. It became darker, and only a dense light above made the path visible. Brian pulled the glow light from his pocket and snapped it. The guide did likewise, pointing to the map; he could see they would soon be crawling through a thin cavern until it broadened at the inner base of the mountain. Two of the men kept watch at the entrance until they were signaled to circle around and cover their tracks.

A jagged rock tore Brian's pant leg, and he could feel the warmth of blood oozing from his skin. It would coagulate. There was no stopping now. The oxygen became thin, and it felt like hours were ticking away as they inched through. He could hear the guide's breath getting shallow. "You okay?"

He grunted, "Yes, almost there."

Brian said a prayer of relief and pushed his pack in front of him into the wider space. He thought, "How did Rojomen make it through here? There has to be another way." The man's eyes opened wide as he gazed upward. There were steps leading up a winding and thin ledge. One slip, and you would fall to your death. He gasped.

"I think this is a test for you my friend. It's time for me to go." He turned to leave.

"You've got to be kidding me. You are leaving me? How do you know I'll make it?" Brian's temper was rising. "After all I've done for the people in this country, that wasn't test enough?"

"Your path is clearly marked now. You no longer need my assistance. Climb, my friend; you need to make it before the sun sets. Unfriendly creatures inhabit this place at night." The man chuckled.

"Is this a game to you? Wait. My wife!" Brian pleaded.

"If I don't hear from Rojomen by tomorrow's end, he will notify Maria of your demise." He disappeared into the dark pathway.

"Thanks a lot!" Brian took a deep breath and prayed. "One foot at a time, Jesus. We can do this. No big deal, like scaling the cliffs at Saguaro Lake." He put the glow stick between his teeth, secured his back pack, and began his ascent some 6,000 feet high. The hours crept slowly by. If he made it to the top it would be nightfall, but he refused to focus on that. The beast flashed before his eyes, but he quickly cast the thought to the bottom of the earth beneath him. He focused on his mental picture of holding Angel in his arms again. His foot slipped, and he hung from the edge of the step.

"Oh God, I'm feet from the top. Don't let me die now." He felt a surge of energy course through his body, and it felt as if a hand gently pulled him up by his shoulders. In moments he lunged to the opening and into the fresh air. "Thank you, Lord."

As he lay prostrate on the ground, he sensed a presence lingering in the woods. Fear welled up within him. He crawled over and perched behind a bush. A firm hand gripped his shoulder, and he almost passed out. He peered up into the eyes of one of the men from the search party. He made a bird call, and the others came out from their hiding.

"Good job!" the translator said as he patted him on the back. The others did likewise. "We must head due east."

All of a sudden, they were surrounded by men shouting in thick foreign accents. One of the men with Brian stepped in front of the other tribal leader. He spoke in their same tongue and the weapons came down. Rojomen sent a search party from another tribe to find them.

Brian asked about Angel's whereabouts and safety. The man assured him that the chief's granddaughter, the princess, was in excellent care. At that moment, the realization that Angel could be taken from their lives forever hit Brian like a tsunami. He collapsed on the ground. The exhaustion of this journey was catching up to him; up to this point, the adrenaline of finding his daughter kept him going.

The men stared at him in disbelief. "He is weak from the journey and taking care of the sick villagers," one replied.

Brian was silent for a few moments as he sat bowed in a heap on the moist ground. Then he remembered the words Rojomen spoke to them when he first brought the child on that cold Christmas night. They reverberated in his head like an old song, "You will never see her again; she will be given a potion to wipe her memory of you. This must be so she can rule our people." He wept.

"This cannot be the time; surely her father wants to meet her and the man who has raised her, the man whose heart she held," he mumbled.

The men got on each side of Brian and brought him to his feet. "We must go. Can you walk?" the kinder of the two men asked.

"Yes." Brian smiled weakly.

They headed into the last leg of their journey, to Rojomen's village. Brian felt safe amidst the strong, muscular warriors, and a peace washed over him. As they entered the village, a host of people came out singing a song. A little child jumped from a lady's arms and ran toward Brian. She wore beaded bracelets, a necklace, a turquoise and amethyst dress, and a crystal tiara.

"Daddy! Daddy! Daddy!" Angel wrapped her arms around his waist.

He lifted her to him, hugging her tightly against his chest. Brian's insides ached at seeing her in native dress. His heart was overwhelmed at God's goodness and torn at the lingering questions about this possibly being the last time he would see his daughter. How would he tell Maria?

Rojomen came up and placed a gentle, but firm hand on Brian's shoulder. It was as if he read his mind. He whispered, "Shalom."

His fears were calmed for the moment, and he would bask in the glory of their safety. Angel slipped out of his arms and grabbed his hand.

"Come, follow me," she said playfully.

She led him to a hut furnished lavishly with African throws. Pearl beads hung from the ceiling surrounding the pillow-covered bed. There was a small table lavished with fruit and nuts.

"These are delicious," she said as she handed him a piece of orange and red mango.

Rojomen followed them along with a portly woman. "This is Rasha; she is Angel's nurse, or as you say in America, nanny."

She bowed her head to Brian.

"Thank you for taking care of my little girl." Brian extended his hand. It surprised him that Rasha responded in English, "You are welcome."

Rojomen explained, "I taught her and several of my people English. The chief's son whom you will meet tomorrow has picked up a little. His father does not speak it well. Therefore, he will speak in our native tongue, and I'll translate."

Chapter Twelve
HIDDEN TREASURES

Eula and Maria walked around the lake. A bald eagle soared above them with its white head and tail glistening in the sunshine. Barbie strolled at a slower pace, snapping pictures of the wildflowers and ducks along the way.

The twins were awake and cooing at the mountain breeze. Joshua ran in the grass with Alesha following close behind him.

"Mom, thanks for coming. It's funny; no one was available last week. Now here you all are. I am grateful. I need the support. You know how sometimes things aren't quiet what they seem. There has been something I've wanted to tell you for a long time." They stopped on the wooden bridge, distracted by the water flowing underneath it from the drainage pipe upstream. It was hidden behind the greenery and rock. "I still don't know if the timing is right. I've been under a lot of stress; my emotions are jumbled up inside." Maria touched her mom's arm.

"See that tiny puddle of water over there. Look at the two ducks playing in it. They have this big lake, and they settle for that. Don't we do the same thing? God offers us everything, and we settle for the little. There are hidden treasures all around us, lessons we can gleam from every day and even in the heartache of life. We have to choose to look for the meaning and purpose in the joy and the chaos. I'm okay with not knowing. You do whatever God is leading your heart to do," Eula empathized.

"You get wiser all the time. Thanks." Maria hugged her mom.

As they walked around to the center of the lake with its artificial waterfalls, the turquoise water bubbled over the rocks. Yellow and black dotted baby ducks swam to the edge of where the water poured out over the rock and rode its current out into the foamy, bubbly stream ending near the water's edge. As soon as they were a little way out, they paddled as fast as they could and did it again. Maria and her mom looked at each other and began to laugh.

Barbie came up behind them, "What's so funny? I got some great pictures of the osprey. See. He's gorgeous, or she. The brown wings and white chest with the inside feathers detailed to match the rest of the coloring perfectly. Anyone who doesn't believe in the detail of our Creator needs to take a look at this bird. Majestic wingspan. This will make a perfect picture for my new house," she said.

Maria pointed to the ducks in the water and nudged Barbie. The mama was overseeing her chicks.

"Oh, my goodness. Won't you look at that? It reminds me of when we used to ride the log ride. We would get soaked and go right back at it. We must have ridden that thing a hundred times back then." She pulled out her camera and started shooting.

"I remember that," Eula responded. "I thought you were going to catch your death by pneumonia because the water was freezing."

They all laughed.

"I snapped some good pictures of Joshua for you," Barbie said as she rubbed Maria's back. "Sorry I was out of touch a few weeks. But hey, I am a fiancée now!" She flared her hand out, showing the sparkling diamond on her finger.

"Congratulations!" they said simultaneously.

"Group hug." Maria pulled them both close to her.

Allon started to cry.

"Ahh. Do you want to be included too?" Barbie picked him up, snuggling him close to her.

"When is the big day?" Eula asked.

"We haven't picked one yet, but you'll be the first to know," Barbie answered.

"Hey." Maria bumped her. "I'm your best friend, right?" She pushed her lip out.

"Of course, you'll be my maid of honor. Joshua will carry the rings. Angel my flower girl," Barbie replied.

Maria started to cry. She sat down on the bench, took Abbie out of the stroller and rocked back and forth. Her mom knelt down beside her, and Barbie sat next to her.

"Ok, what gives?" Barbie asked.

Maria looked into her mother's eyes. "I'm worried sick Angel won't come back with Brian."

"Oh, sweetie, Jesus will bring both of them home. He will," her mom assured.

Joshua came running up and handed Maria a purple flower. It seemed like he went from toddling around to walking and running in a matter of days. He was a quick learner and would not stop until his head hit the pillow.

"Thank you, my sweet boy. Mommy loves you this much, and she stretched her arm out long." Abbie stirred in her other arm.

"Here, let me take her. You go play with him awhile. Alesha and Barbie will walk with me," Eula instructed.

Alesha replied, "Actually, I've been called into work. Someone called out. I need to close tonight. Pita Jungle awaits. The tips are a great way to pay for nursing school. Will either of you be sticking around to help Maria?"

"I can stay until tomorrow. She needs the company," Barbie responded.

"Great. Thanks. See you later." Alesha bounded out to her car.

Maria followed Joshua around the park.

"I want us to pray with her before I leave. Aaron is back at Maria's house watching the game. We have to catch a flight to Dallas tomorrow. Please keep an eye on her. I know you are busy finishing up your Master's and planning a wedding, but I'm concerned about her," Eula commented.

"I know, Mom. I will. I promise," Barbie assured Eula.

"Thank you. Isn't it amazing this lake is hidden from the world's eyes behind the mountains, trees, and these houses? Yet, it holds a multitude of riches for us to enjoy. The eagle, osprey, ducks, and geese live from the bounty underneath the water's surface. The lessons we can learn by observing the creation are endless. The Father has provided them all, sweet hidden treasures for the eyes that choose to see," Eula stated.

Chapter Thirteen
VEILED TRUTH

As Brian lay under the thatched roof with Angel snuggled up beside him, the miombo trees swayed, touching the sides of the mud hut. These trees reminded Brian of the large oak trees he climbed when visiting Alabama over the summer as a child. He could hear the monkeys singing and chattering nonstop in the background. It sounded like the flocks of quail wandering up and down the Queen Valley Golf Course. He and his dad played there often. Those memories ran through his mind as clear as if they were yesterday.

His father would pick him up from middle school and head straight to the course. The manager knew them by name and would let them play until dark. After they hit a round of nine holes, his dad would say, "Okay, Son, it's getting dark. Are you ready to go explore the trail now?"

He was always ready to end the golf lessons because of the life lessons his dad would give. "Put your whole heart into it. Follow it through," Brian could hear him bellow. These laid the foundation for the man Brian became.

Once the sun began to set, they would walk the paved path up and down the hills along the green carpet on either side. The pond glistened as the sun's final rays played across the top. Before their walk ended, you could hear the quail crowing and coyotes howling on their rampage in the deep ditch that separated the duplexes from the course. Every once in a while, a jet-black tarantula would creep across their path, or a lizard would scurry up a rock. Most nights the trail would be scattered with cotton tails in abundance.

At the beginning of summer his dad's playful side would kick in. He would grab Brian's hand and pull him toward the sprinklers. When the water cascaded into one of the road signs making the sound of a rattler, his eyes would grow big, and his dad would push him out of the way, pretending to get bit. His dad would fall to the ground and laugh hysterically.

These were the times Brian cherished and missed the most. His dad traveled for work a lot, but he was present when he was home.

Angel stirred beside him, and Brian pulled the blanket closer to her face, tucking it around her. Then he crept out the door to gaze at the midnight darkness and the Milky Way above. A shooting star penetrated the night.

"Lord, the Bible says, we are but a vapor, much like that star, here for a little while and gone. I don't know how much time I have on this planet, but make it count for your glory, not my own. Bless Maria and my children while I'm away; protect them and provide for their needs. Bring in the other children from the vision you gave to me after Isaiah passed, in your time, Lord. Thank you," he prayed.

Brian heard rumbling in the bushes and a boar broke through the thick weeds, charging straight for him. He dodged just in time. Panting heavily, the large creature with red eyes turned to face him. Before he could think of what to do, Angel appeared in the doorway hollering for him.

"No!" he yelled as the animal turned toward her voice. "Angel!" Brian ran toward her. In a split second, with precise accuracy, an arrow whizzed past his head and hit the boar, piercing through its tough skin, bringing it crashing to the ground in front of the child's feet.

Angel cried. Brian scooped her up into his arms. The night watchman eyed Brian suspiciously, saying something in their native tongue. All he could do was say, "Thank you."

The man heaved the creature out of the way and pointed to the entry sharply. This small gesture was enough, and they obeyed instantly. Later Brian could hear the sound of feet shuffling in the darkness. He knew they must be skinning the beast for roasting. One thing he had learned during this trip, the people here did not waste anything. They used every resource the woodland provided: firewood, charcoal, timber, thatching grass, medicines, fruit, honey, and even beasts.

They saw many wild animals on this trip: the long, stately walk of the orange giraffes, the enormous grey elephants with their babies tucked between the herd to protect them from predators, the endless scores of blackened chimpanzees, wrinkle-skinned rhinos, and the small brown monkeys swinging in the trees. Thank God, they had not encountered any gorillas. Brian heard the guide talk about their massive size and aggressive behavior.

He could not help but wonder what else hid in this mysterious land and jungle mist. He thought the eyes of the pig looked almost demonic glowing in the night. He shuttered and pulled Angel closer to him. This territory was definitely out of his league, but he trusted the Father and Rojomen to keep them safe.

Morning came way too early as Brian's fitful tossing and turning never allowed him to reach REM. He dreamt the fierce winds of the Neatorama hurricane tore Maria and his children from his arms, while the piercing eyes, and massive paws of its creature waited to pounce on them. He had overcome the trauma experienced on Neatorama Island, but it took a lot of work with his psychiatrist. He shook himself awake and prayed release from the fear trying to envelope him like fog in a valley.

"Good morning," Rojomen's gentle, but strong voice called.

"Come in. We aren't quite up yet," Brian responded.

At the sound of his voice, Angel sat up and rubbed her sleepy eyes. She crawled up on Brian's lap and buried her face into his chest. He wrapped his arms around her.

"I would like to go over today's procedures with you. In about an hour, when you see the sun making its way just above those treetops, Angel must be dressed in her royal attire. You'll wear this." He handed Brian a three-quarter length exquisitely fashioned robe and pants. "Two of the chief's guards will come to escort you and present you to Angel's grandfather and father. The old man's eyesight is dim, but he'll hear your words as I translate them. Bow before them as you enter the room. I'll nod when you may speak. This is a great honor. - Do you understand?" Rojomen asked.

"Yes, but I don't understand." He looked at Angel, judging whether to continue. "This scenario is nothing like what you told Maria and me.

Rojomen smiled and said, "Everything will be explained. Trust me." He winked as he looked affectionately at the little girl curled up in her father's lap.

Angel tried bringing her long-curled eyelashes together back at him. Rojomen laughed. Brian felt a calm assurance rush over him.

"Remember my friend, things aren't always as they appear," he said as he exited the hut.

"Angel, we must get ready." A bowl of warm water was brought in by the woman who previously cared for Angel.

Brian said, "I'll do it. Thank you."

"No, not so in our culture. Come, Angel." She reached out her hands to the child and Angel kissed her dad on the cheek and diligently obeyed.

"It's okay, Daddy. She's taken good care of me," Angel replied.

Brian nodded, trying to force the knot in his throat down. The nanny pinned a blanket up between them. He dressed in the formal native clothing Rojomen left for him. The long turquoise was intricately embroidered from one end to the other with white flowers. The sash about his neck was purple. He washed his face and combed his hair.

"May I see my princess now?" Brian challenged.

Angel peeped her head around the corner. "Do you want to watch her do my hair? Maybe you can learn to do it this way, so we can show Mommy. It's cool."

"Okay, sounds good." A tear trickled down his face, and he turned quickly to wipe it away.

The lady wove flowers with a purple ribbon through Angel's hair with great care. She placed the tiara on her head. Brian noticed that the colors in his garment were identical to Angel's. He contemplated their meaning. Pink and red flowers dotted her thick braids and stood out against the ebony of her hair.

"You look lovely, Princess," Brian said as he took a bow. They had played princess and the castle many times. He had even built her a miniature castle in their back yard with an ivory-painted tower splashed with pink hearts.

"Your mama would be proud of you and how brave you've been." Brian hugged her.

"I miss her." Angel teared up.

"No crying now," Nanny said. "We don't want to ruin this special time."

She knew how hard this day would be for the chief's son. They were celebrating his return to his people and his healing from near death; it was a bittersweet event. Her heart ached for this man she had once loved. Tending to his children was the greatest gift she could ask for.

Neither Brian nor Angel had any realization of the magnitude of what was about to happen. The two escorts arrived as the crystal dawn of morning revealed itself, peaking above the tall, oak-looking trees. There were hundreds of different types of miombo bushes and trees scattered throughout the woodland. The native people used them for every purpose.

As he peered up into the sky he said, "I'd love to do some research here." His research had come to a stall with the ban on using the flower from Neatorama. He did not understand how the board could be so pig-headed. He showed ample proof of the effects it had on cancer cells. One desperate mom was willing to let him use an experimental dose on her dying daughter, and even though he had her sign a paper releasing the hospital from all responsibility, they denied usage of the natural medicine without more scientific evidence. His blood boiled once again as he thought of the little girl in the casket and her grieving mother. A white and orange striped butterfly flew above his head as if to say, "Remember who is in control."

"Okay, Lord. I release it to you. It's not over yet. You make a way." Brian took in a deep breath and let it out slowly.

They came to a clearing in the forest. A massive tent lay before them with silk draperies pegged on eight sides. A path of fuchsia petals lay strewn on the dirt trail leading to the entrance. Warriors held spears in the form of an arch that made a canopy over Angel and Brian who bowed in honor. Drums echoed their rhythmic sound.

Brian wanted to grab Angel and run. His heart trembled with fear for what he was about to lose. On the inside he prayed, "Father, help me be strong. We promised Lord, but I don't know if I can do this. I don't know if I can let her go." He felt his heart beating more quickly and his palms sweating. He looked down at his beautiful child. "Father, your will be done. I surrender to you." He breathed deep in and out for ten seconds.

Rojomen walked up behind him and placed his hand on Brian's back. "Are you ready?" he asked.

Brian shook his head no.

"Trust me," Rojomen whispered.

They made the procession down the pathway. Rojomen introduced them, "Princess Angel and Guardian Brian."

Angel started to speak, but Rojomen put his hand over his mouth as a gesture to silence her. They walked slowly up to the three thrones facing a lovely, elegant woman, a white-bearded and weathered man, and a middle-aged man with deep scars from the right side of his face protruding down his neck with a crown of gold and silver matching Angel's tiara. Each one wore similar clothing. Atop the lady's head was a double-sized tiara like Angel's. Next to the woman, there appeared to be a bassinet covered in shimmering crystals and pearls with a silk tapestry above it.

Brian took Angel's hand, and they bowed before them.

Rojomen interpreted as the chief spoke, "You may rise. Many years ago, when our country was in the midst of turbulent times, I made a promise to my son that I would protect his only child, a little girl, who would become heir to her father's throne. Angel, come here child." He pointed to her and motioned for her to come to him.

Brian urged her. He took her by the hand and led her to the man.

The old man embraced her and wept on her shoulder. I am your grandfather. I never thought I would live to see this day."

Angel's tender and compassionate nature could not resist returning his affection.

He then released her. "Go stand with Brian."

Then the younger man spoke, "I want to thank you for taking care of my little girl. You have done a marvelous job. All the while in the prison camp and during the horrific torture, her infant face kept me alive. Your prayers and our God delivered me, along with my faithful servant." He looked at Rojomen and put his hand to his chest. "They never gave up their search to find me." He held out his arms to Angel. The child drew back to Brian. Looking up into his eyes, hers filled with tears as she focused on him. His heart was about to burst.

She cried as she clung to his leg, "You are my daddy."

Brian knelt and held her, "Yes child, by choice I am. I love you more than life itself. But this man is your father too, and he gave you to me to protect you. He won't hurt you. Go to him."

"Please, child. I've waited a long time." His longing and gentle voice compelled her, and she ran to him.

He hugged her long and hard. Rojomen commanded all the servants to leave the tent. Tears poured from the eyes of all seated on the thrones.

Brian's mind raced. How will we recover? We've lost so much already. Fear overwhelmed his heart.

Rojomen sensed his apprehension and put his arm around Brian's shoulder.

The chief's son commanded, "Brian, come here." He put Angel over to his lady's side. She embraced her. He held Brian and kept repeating, "Thank you. Thank you. Thank you." Then he introduced Brian to his bride, the lady to his right.

Rojomen gently went to the cradle and picked up a swaddled infant. He handed the bundle to his master.

"This is Prince Taj, and his name means "exalted or crown." He is Angel's brother," Rojomen translated.

Angel rushed over to the child, eyes wide with excitement. "I've always wanted a baby brother or sister that looked like me!" she squealed.

Brian's knees buckled, and he almost collapsed.

The chief spoke to his wife in their native tongue. She stood, bowed, took the baby and Angel's hand, and led them to the door.

"Wait," Brian called.

Angel jerked loose and rushed to his side, "It's okay, Daddy. It's okay. I'll be right back." She hugged him tight.

He knelt and embraced her. As she turned and walked away, he said, "I love you to the moon and back, my little princess." Tears stung his cheeks as she looked back and waved bye. He let her go, but his heart yearned to grab her and scream, "No!" His flight mechanism was about to kick in when Rojomen grabbed him by the hand and pulled him to his feet.

"Stay with me, my friend. We are not through here," he spoke gently.

Brian's eyes glazed over with grief as he stared at the two men. He did not want to hear anymore, so he thought.

Maria sat at Bergies Coffee Roast house in Gilbert. She had purposefully chosen two seats up on the stage, so she could see when her company would arrive. Peach-faced love birds chirped merrily in the trees. It was a miracle Eula and Barbie were available to watch the children. Her mind raced with questions about why Beatrice would want to meet with her. Why did she want to meet alone and in public? Would she fight to keep Joshua away from them? Each week had been a battle of wills. The judge ordered them to take turns bringing Joshua to specified locations, but Beatrice needed control and would do whatever it took to get it.

Just last week, she changed their scheduled day last minute, causing upheaval as Maria had to rearrange entire days to oblige her demands. Did she have any idea how hard it was for her to get three children ready and to a sitter three-and-a-half hours away? Did she even care?

Maria began to stew, her cheeks glowed bright red, and she felt sick. "Brian come home," she pleaded internally.

Beatrice appeared with her head high, strutting like a peacock, with her briefcase in hand. As Maria looked at her, something seemed different. She did not seem disheveled; her nails were polished a soft lavender, and her hair was softly pulled up into a loose bun.

Maria stood and choose her words carefully, "You look amazing."

"Thank you, dear." Beatrice replied. "I'm sorry I had you drive this far. I know it must have been difficult."

Maria's mouth dropped open. She thought, "Is she toying with me." Beatrice never, ever apologized. Maria was stunned. It took her a minute to respond, but she finally blurted out, "Thank you."

"This is a lovely place," Beatrice said as she looked around admiring the flowers and birds.

"Yes, it's my favorite coffee shop in the area. Brian and I used to come study here when we were dating."

"Would you like a coffee?" Beatrice asked.

Maria had completely forgotten to order her normal chai. Her hands clutched in her lap to keep them from shaking. "I would love a chai with almond milk. Thank you."

Beatrice laid her briefcase on the chair across from Maria. "I'll be right back then."

"Wow, non-confrontational, that's a first." Maria breathed a sigh of relief until she glanced at the black shiny case staring at her. "What does she have in there? Did she have the upper hand, and she knew it? Is that why she's so calm?" She started to hyperventilate but remembered the breathing techniques and mindfulness instructions. "Okay, girl, bring that train in, and get off it now!" she told herself. During her stay at the psychiatric hospital after Isaiah's death, she learned that thoughts are like trains, and you have to learn not to board them sometimes.

Maria prayed silently, "Jesus, please don't let them take our visitation rights away."

Beatrice walked up, "Oh dear, you look flush. Are you okay?" she asked handing Maria her drink.

"Yes, I'm fine," she snapped.

Beatrice sat her drink on the mosaic tile table between them. Then she reached to give Maria a hug. "Everything is going to be okay."

She did not know what to say. This was completely out of character for Beatrice. Maria could hardly concentrate. Her eyebrows raised instinctively.

"This coffee is delicious. Let's get down to business," Beatrice smiled.

"Oh no you didn't," Maria thought. "Here it comes. I knew it. This was all a façade." Battle walls back up. The briefcase slid across the table in front of them. As each clip unsnapped Maria felt more nauseated.

She abruptly stood up. "I need to go to the restroom," she stammered.

"Maria, it's okay." Beatrice stood, but she was already around the corner and in the door.

Maria rushed past the guest in line, excusing herself, with a cupped hand over her mouth. She went in, shut and locked the bathroom door, splashed cold water on her face, and sat on the toilet. "Daddy, I can't do this. I need Brian and Angel. Please, don't let me lose both of my babies. I can't bear anymore." She wailed with her face in her hands. She tried to muffle her sobs with the wet paper towel.

A soft voice called outside the door. "Maria, are you okay?" Beatrice sounded genuinely concerned. "Look, I don't want to talk this way, but you're wrong in what you're thinking. I just want to be a grandma to Joshua. I can't be his mom; you are. My daughter knew that. I've actually been praying. I know it's hard for you to believe. We want you and Brian to have custody of Joshua. We want visitation rights. Here are the papers. I had my lawyer draw them up." She slid them under the door.

"I'll be waiting outside." Her heels clicked away.

Maria reached for the papers, and with trembling hands began to read. "Oh, my word. God, thank you. Thank you, Father." She wept joyfully.

She slung the bathroom door open, not caring how rosy her nose and cheeks were. Her legs could not walk fast enough to where

Beatrice sat. Maria wrapped her arms around her. They embraced for the first time ever, and Maria felt they finally crossed the threshold from enemies to friends.

"I owe you an apology. I've always been a harsh person. It's the way I was raised. My mama always told me, "Life is hard. You got to take care of you." It became my vision; it was all I could see. After Adaline died, I realized how wrong I was. I thought I could make up for it by fighting for Joshua. I was wrong again. I want to change. I don't want to try and fix the past. I want to make things right in the present. I want us to be friends. My husband and I want to be good grandparents. I don't know how to be either. Maria, will you help me?"

"Yes, yes. I've prayed for this moment for two years." She hugged her. "Adaline would be so proud."

"When will Brian be home?" Beatrice asked.

Maria looked down at her hand, "I don't know. I've been trying not to think about it. I hope soon."

"Either way, these legal documents have been sent to the judge in Flagstaff. The process has begun. I'm sure you'll be hearing from her office soon. You are an amazing woman. I admire you. I could not wish for a better mom for Joshua. I can tell how much you love him by the way you look at him. It's been hard. Thank you." Beatrice took Maria's hand. "We'll come to see him next week. His birthday is soon. Let's plan a party together. I would love to help. One thing I am good at is parties," Beatrice explained.

Maria watched her walk away. She basked in the glorious rays of the sun, taking in the beauty of the day. She knew there would be challenges along the way in their relationship. They were both pretty headstrong, but she felt like this was the beginning of something good, and she had her boy. The birds seemed to pick up on her happy vibes and sang loudly throughout the trees. Maria thought it sounded like they were singing, "Oh, Happy Day".

Chapter Fourteen
JOY UNSPEAKABLE

Rojomen carried a stump over and placed it in front of the two men. "Sit please." He ushered Brian onto the seat.

The older man began to speak, "You've taken great care of the child, raised her well. She's compassionate, caring, and kind. All great traits for a leader of the people. This day is a celebration because my son and granddaughter are reunited. You've fulfilled your promise."

Brian wanted to speak, but his head was dizzy, and words would not come.

"I'm thankful my son has found love again and brought another child into the world, which we did not think would ever be possible. When he came back to us he was near death. It's a miracle from our God. Today is sweet because we have met our Angel. Today is bitter because we must let her go once again," he continued.

Brian cleared his throat, "What did you say?"

The chief with quivering lips repeated what his father said, "We must let her go. We've an heir for our people who will be trained up in our customs. He will be prepared to take his father's place when the time comes," he answered.

Brian fell to his knees and bowed. "Thank you, Lord, Jehovah."

The younger man continued, "Thank you for bringing my daughter. When I first arranged for her to come, I wanted her to remain with us. She is a beautiful portrait of her mother. One night in prayer, as I gazed up at the heavens, I heard a whisper through the wind saying,

"You have your heir with you now. He shall be the prince of your people." He rose and placed his hand on Brian's shoulder. "You've done well, my brother."

The father replied, "Tonight we'll celebrate the goodness of our God, the Heavenly Father who brought you a child from an unknown place and who rescued my son from the jaws of death. We'll savor this precious moment in time with our Angel."

He summoned Brian to him, enclosed his arms around him, and they wept much like Joseph did when he was re-united with his brothers.

Brian's heart swelled with gratitude. "Thank you."

A grand party ensued. They gathered around the fire pit, danced, feasted, and celebrated deep into the night. Angel climbed up into Brian's lap and fell fast asleep. The chief came over to Brian and gently kissed the child on the head.

"We've arranged for you to go home in the morning. Our attention will be placed on protecting the prince. If anything were to happen to him, Angel would be needed again, but we do not anticipate such an event," he informed.

Brian stood and embraced him. "Thank you!" As the man walked away, he turned to Rojomen and said, "May I ask you a question?"

Rojomen nodded yes.

"Did you purposefully send us through the camp with the sickness?"

"No, but our God in His mercy told me to send you that way," he responded.

"I don't know for sure if the medicine worked, if the tribe was cured," Brian challenged.

"You don't always see it. If we saw everything that could happen, we would be paralyzed with fear. The Bible tells us there are more for us than against us. We received word this morning that only two of the sickest died, but all else recovered."

"What about the chieftain's son? Is he alive?" he asked.

"He's alive. Trust. Our lives depend on the five-letter word." Rojomen laughed.

"Will we ever see you again?" Brian looked at him with raised eyebrows.

"I have a family to protect. I'm their guardian, but I'll always be looking out for you, even if you can't see me. There'll be no more threats against your child or family. You've persevered, and you've received the prize," he said as he affectionately touched Angel's head. He patted Brian on the back. "Get some rest. You've a long journey ahead through some of the most breath-taking and treacherous land in Africa."

"One more question. "What was the stair-well climb about?" Brian asked.

"When our boys reach maturity and are going to start a family, they must complete a test of strength, courage, and endurance. You took a child from our tribe into your family yet had not completed our tribal commission. The entire journey from your country to today was your test. You passed. Good job!" Rojomen answered.

Brian sighed with relief. It all felt like a trial, and relief came in knowing it was over.

He carried Angel to their hut and settled her in their bed. As he lay with his eyes looking toward the skies, he felt lighter than he had in a long time. A picture came to his mind. He could see it clearly, like a vision in the night. He floated up in the air and was peering into a room. Maria was in Angel's room rocking one of the babies. The monitor voiced another infant crying in the background. She started to sing a familiar lullaby, and tranquility filled the air, much like the scene in the Bible where Jesus said, "Peace be still," and calmed the sea.

Joshua played at her feet. "Vrrm. Vrrm. Mommy, watch." He took his firetruck over to Angel's baby doll house. "Swoosh. Swoosh. The fire's all out, and everybody's safe."

"Good job, honey," Maria encouraged his active imagination.

Brian wanted to grab and hold them. A light shone on the picture above Maria's head.

"The vision!" He exhaled. He could see it clearly come into focus, the four children and Isaiah playing – it had come to pass.

The meaning of their names danced around in his head: Angel (Messenger), Joshua (Jehovah is generous), Abbie (My Father Rejoices) and little Allon (Strong as an oak).

"Amazing! Lord, Jehovah, you do provide. It's been a rough, jagged road, but my family is complete, and Jesus, you've fulfilled your promise to abundantly restore. My heart is filled with unspeakable joy. Thank you!" Brian expressed.

Aaron and Eula danced up and down and started to sing, "God is so good. God is so good. He's so good to me. God answers prayer. God answers prayer. God answers pray, and he's so good to me." They embraced Maria. Her heart burst with excitement, and she was thankful they were home to share the good news of Beatrice's report.

Her mom replied, "Thanks for bringing the children. We've missed you all."

Aaron swung Joshua up on top of his shoulders, grabbed his hands, and started spinning in a circle. The boy cackled with glee.

"Fantastic! Have you heard from Brian?" Aaron questioned.

She had been avoiding her parents as much as possible because she did not want to answer any of their questions. How could she tell them Angel may not come back? And why, especially since they did not get to say their final goodbyes to her?

"Joshua, it's time to change your diaper. Shuuwee." She pinched her nose and grabbed his hand. She dismissed their longing looks and picked up her son. When she came back from the nursery, the twins lay one in each of her parents' arms. This was not fair to them.

Maria put her best face on. "We should hear from them soon. I have to get back before dark. The pediatrician called and wants to do a follow-up on the twins. I promise to call as soon as I hear from Brian. I'm sure he and Angel are having a great safari adventure." She put Joshua down and took Allon from her mother's arms. "He's so tiny. I worry about him. I know I shouldn't, but I do." Her eyes misted.

Eula could sense the deep sadness in her daughter. "Why don't your dad and I come stay with you for a week or so? This heat is killing me?"

"Yeah, we aren't traveling for a couple of weeks. We'd love to spend time spoiling our grandchildren and give you a break." Aaron threw his arm around her.

"Hmmm." Maria cleared her throat.

"Okay, you too." He smiled. "You're not getting precious Abbie unless you agree."

"Fine, but life's a little crazy right now, and my house is a disaster," Maria countered.

"We aren't coming to see your house, and I can help with that." Eula retorted.

"You win. You might pick up the healthy food you like to eat. My house is filled with baby and toddler foods." Maria laughed.

"You take good care of yourself and family, my friend." Rojomen hugged Brian. "This is where I leave you."

The two men embraced. Brian did not want to let go. He felt as if this was the last time he would see him. Rojomen's strong and lingering hug told his heart it was so.

"The men will get you to the convoy at the edge of the Congo where the entourage will pick you up and take you safely inland. Keep your eyes and hears open. Protect the child with your life. I know you will." He turned to Angel and knelt down in front of her. "May I have a hug, young princess?"

She nodded and threw her arms around him, "You've always been there. Haven't you?"

He smiled and said, "Yes, child, I have."

"Don't forget us," she said.

"Never!" Rojomen responded.

She kissed his cheek and grabbed Brian's hand. "I'm ready to go home."

She looked up at her daddy, and in that moment, he was taken back in time to a snow-driven cabin on Christmas Eve, when he was given the choice to open his heart to a perfect baby girl. "I'm so glad I did," he said out loud.

Angel looked back and waved into the darkness of the forest as Rojomen had already disappeared. During their preparation time, he had given them strict instructions to talk quietly, if they must, stop only as needed, and follow their guides implicitly.

As the company traversed through the woods, Brian's thoughts meandered home. Maria must be terrified. They had been gone for weeks already, and it would take them two to three days to meet up with the convoy.

Suddenly, there was something like an earthquake; something large was moving their way. Brian grabbed Angel and followed the men into the opening that led out to a sandy beach area.

"Run! Run! Run!" the commander yelled.

The massive heads and grey trunks of the elephants swung wildly; the cracking and popping of branches echoed through the forests as the heard stampeded in their direction.

"To the water!" hollered one of the men.

They followed without hesitation; the mighty creatures' breath was upon them. The men behind Brian yelled and screamed, waving their spears in the air.

"Oh God, help us!" Brian prayed. Angel clung to him in terror. They were chest level in the waters of the Pacific, and he propelled her to his shoulders. He covered the child's eyes as the elephants were about to crush one of the men, but in an instant, they turned. The man collapsed in the sand. The rest thrust their weapons in the air in jubilant victory.

They hollered, "Praise to the King! Praise to the King!"

Brian walked to the shallow water and pulled Angel down to his chest. She was crying.

"It's okay, we are safe. What an adventure. Remember when we play castle at home? On this journey, let's pretend we are fighting off the enemy, look for wonders like the ginormous elephants, and explore new things. We've never seen anything like that at the zoo, have we?" Brian encouraged.

"No. Okay, I'll be brave," Angel whimpered.

A brightly orange, black, and yellow-striped fish swam close to his legs. "Look, a new discovery," he said as he pointed into the water."

"It's beautiful!" she exclaimed. "It almost looks like our fish in my aquarium at home."

Her eyes misted over, "I miss Mommy, Joshua, and the babies."

"I know, honey. I do too," he comforted.

Abruptly, the man who was laying on the shore stood up and then toppled over.

"Something is wrong. Let's go." He rushed to the shore, put Angel down, and kneeled by the man's side. Brian began checking his pulse. He called out to the leader, "Find my bag!"

In their haste to escape he had thrown it into the brush. The men scattered to look for it.

"He must be in shock." Brian shook the man. "Where are you hurting? Can you hear me?" He looked at the terrorized face of his daughter. "It's okay, honey. Pray."

The sweet girl came over and laid her hands on the man's chest, and with great authority said, "Jesus heal this man who saved us from the elephants, in Jesus name!"

Brian began to exam each inch of the man's body. On his lower leg was a hole. "This is it. The elephant's tusk must have got him. We need to clean and bandage it," he told the leader.

Everything in Brian's bag was crushed, except for a few gauze strips and powdered electrolyte packs. "Thank you, Jesus. Thank you, sweetie." He sterilized the wound with water and began wrapping it.

"Wait, use these. The powder will fight off any infection and help the laceration to heal." Rojomen's brother used a rock to crush the miombo leaves and handed them to Brian.

"Thank you. Will you hold his foot and here on his leg? This will stabilize it." He pointed to just above the man's calf muscle. He turned to his daughter. "Angel, why don't you sing your lullaby?"

The young girl sang a melodic chorus as the men went about bandaging the injury. Then Brian took the canister of water hanging over his shoulder, mixed in the nutrients, and held it to the man's lips. He did not respond. He motioned for the commander of the group to come over.

"They will need to carry him or create a hoist to pull him," Brian instructed.

The tallest and strongest man cut limbs with his machete and wove leaves together to make a travois. Two of the men went fishing for food, and the others made a fire to cook the bounty.

"We'll rest here tonight. Move tomorrow," the leader commanded.

Brian checked on the middle-aged man with wrinkled skin and gentle eyes several times through the night. The others took shifts guarding the camp until morning light. The eerie stillness of the night against the backdrop of the brightly lit stars and crescent moon shimmering off the calmness of the ocean lulled Brian into a deep sleep.

He drifted into another time and place. His mind fixed on the Neatorama island, the lurking beast in the tree line with thick smoking swirls cascading from its nostrils like an overflowing waterfall. The vision appeared clear as day, and he watched helplessly as it pounced on the man standing on the rock. He could see the terror-stricken face of the man as the massive paw hurled him into the air.

Angel shook Brian. "Daddy! Daddy! Are you okay? Wake up, wake up."

His eyes popped open. Angel glared at him.

"Yes, it's okay. Only a nightmare." Brian cleared his throat.

One of the guards came over. "You okay?"

"Yes, thank you," he answered.

"Morning's light." He pointed to the ocean.

The sun peeped halfway above the water's edge. It looked as if it was being birthed from the womb of the ocean.

"We'll move soon. There is one day's journey to meet the convoy, if we travel fast and light. We'll follow the beach until it ends around the rock wall. See there?"

"Yes," Brian responded.

One of the men Brian and Angel became quite fond of, Rojomen's brother, lifted Angel to his broad shoulders and smiled. "I must protect the princess," he said, lifting his make-believe sword into the air and bowing.

She laughed. "Thank you, my hero."

The troop walked for several miles following the ocean's shore, but then cut north after climbing the trail up the side of a rocky cliff. The men scaled the side like the mountain goats on Bush Highway by Saguaro Lake, but Brian came near certain death or by impalement a couple of times. Thanks to the immediate responses of the men below and in front of him, he was saved. Sweat trickled down his forehead into his eyes.

"Come on, Daddy. You got this. You can do it!" Brian's own words echoed back at him through his child.

"Yes, I can," he said.

As he reached the top, a massive hand extended toward him, Brian reached out and grabbed it. It pulled him to the top. He breathed heavily a sigh of relief and thankfulness as he looked at the gorgeous view behind him. The scene contrasted the fears he must face going back into the dark jungle before him. The old files from past journeys must be latched closed, if he was to continue his voyage toward home with the gift of his precious daughter; she was approaching her seventh birthday.

Sitting on the rock peering over the ravine, sipping water and catching his breath, Brian was reminded that seven is the number of completion. Seven years ago, was the beginning of his journey as a father, and this year would be the culmination of the vision. He knew his heavenly Father to be the God of the impossible, and he prayed their family would finally be complete.

The first part of the drive toward home was showered with saguaros crowned with delicate white flowers that the birds could feast from as the bees buzzed above them. Then as Maria drove along, the mountains began to look more rounded and tipped in the distance. She sat in awe of the vast difference in the landscape from Phoenix to Flagstaff; it changed at least five times.

As she drove, her mind began to race, "Why did the doctor want to see the twins now?" The deep, somber tone in his voice told her something was wrong. Rain drops began to dance lightly across the windshield, and within minutes she was driving through a torrential downpour. The monsoon season thus far had only consisted of dangerously aggressive dust storms sweeping through the valley and light rains in the mountains with high winds. Tonight, proved differently.

All of the children were asleep in the back seats, and she felt grateful for it. "Father God, get my parents and us safely home. Please, let me hear from Brian soon, and keep them safe. Let the twins be okay and the report be good or give me the strength and back to carry it. Thank you."

Maria could barely see the road. Their appointment was scheduled for 8:00 a.m. It was well past 7 pm now. In this storm she drove at a snail's pace and kept her eyes peeled for the elk and deer inhabiting this region in droves. More than once they had nearly hit one. Her white knuckles clenched the steering wheel, and she took deep breaths to calm herself. She could almost feel Brian's gentle hands pressing against her shoulders, massaging the tension away, and her body relaxing.

"Siri, call mom," she commanded. This startled Allon, and he began to cry. "Shhh. It's okay, honey."

"Hello. You home?" Eula said as she looked at her caller ID.

"No, I suggest you wait until the morning to come. A storm hit, and there maybe flooding tonight. We're about ten or so miles out," Maria voiced.

"Yeah, your dad picked it up on the weather cam. What time do you need us there?" Eula asked.

"If you could be here by 7:00 a.m., that would be great. Dad can stay with Joshua and you can come with me, if you want?"

Allon woke Abbie and Joshua with his squeaky mouse cries. Abbie was mad. Joshua asked, "Mommy, are we there yet?" and covered his ears.

"I'll let you go. See you in the morning. I love you all," Eula said.

"We're pulling up now. Thanks." Maria pushed the garage door opener; nothing happened. The outside lights were on a timer, and they weren't on either.

"Well, this is creepy," she commented.

"What mommy?" Joshua's eyes filled with tears.

"It's okay. Let's sing, God is bigger than the boogie man!" she comforted.

His eyes grew wide and lit up. They began to sing. Maria dialed her neighbor's number.

"Hi, Beth. I'm sorry to be calling late. Is your power off?" Maria questioned.

"Yes, it is. Did you just get home?" Beth inquired.

"Yeah, and my garage door won't open. I haven't used the generator in months, and I don't know if it has gas." She said flabbergasted.

"I'll be right over. Ger, let's go help Maria!" she hollered to her son.

"Thank you," Maria said.

The lanky, blonde, late teen held the large flashlight in one hand and an umbrella in another. "Do you want me to call Ash?" he asked. "Looks like you could use her help." He smiled from ear to ear.

"No, but thanks." She winked at him.

For a moment, Maria's thoughts wandered off to the first time she met Alesha. She was no longer the frazzled young girl they met a few years ago at the Flagstaff coffee shop. The loss of her baby girl almost destroyed her, but she gave her life to Jesus and reunited with her parents. She had allowed the Lord to do a remarkable amount of healing in her life.

Alesha and Ger, short for Gerrett, had been dating a few months now. He was a respectful young man and loved children. She was a couple of years older than him, but Maria was happy they hit it off. Beth unbuckled Joshua, while Ger opened the front door and made sure the house was safe. His dad had taught him well. Beth's husband was a combat soldier killed in Iraq a few years prior.

Maria carried Allon and Abbie in each hand, gripping the handles of their infant seats tightly. They were getting heavier.

"Look at you, muscle woman," Beth joked. She snuggled Joshua under her raincoat. The women hurried inside trying to shield the children as much as possible from the heavy rain drops.

Ger managed to get the generator going. "That should do until tomorrow, if you get everyone in bed by 9:00 and use the oil lamps I found after that."

"Great. Thanks," Maria replied.

Joshua tugged on his pant leg. "Story, please?"

"After you put your PJ's on and go to the potty. He's almost potty trained, or he was until he went to stay with Beatrice and Frederick, but that's all behind us now." She dismissed the negativity running through her tired mind. "You okay reading him a story?" she asked Ger.

"Yes, I can stay a little longer. Mom, would you like me to walk you home first?" He turned to Beth.

Terror filled her eyes.

"You can stay too, Beth. I would love the company." Maria dispelled her fears.

Thunder and lightning cracked and flashed outside the kitchen window. Maria and Beth each took a baby, changed and fed them while Ger tended to Joshua. The house fell peacefully quiet.

Maria made them both a cup of tea.

"Sorry for my reaction. Since Tom passed away I can't handle being alone during the storms," Beth apologized.

"Don't apologize. I'm glad you stayed," Maria said as she patted her hand. "I'd love to get to know you more. Life's been busy."

"I'm going to light the lamps, turn off the generator, and then go home. I need to study," Ger said as he entered the room.

Surprised by his comment, Maria questioned, "I thought you were off school for the summer?"

He smiled sheepishly. "I'm taking summer courses at the college; I would like to graduate early and finish up my senior year with my Associates degree already in hand. When my dad died, my world was turned upside down and it put me behind a year. I'm making up for lost time." He turned to his mom. "I'll come back for you when you're ready."

"You are a wonderful and courteous young man. I'm proud of you." Maria slapped him on the back.

"I'll come now. I'm kind of tired. It was good talking to you. Let us know if you need anything." Beth patted Maria on the shoulder.

"I'll walk you to the door. I need to lock the dead bolt anyway." Maria wrapped one arm around each of them. "You're the best neighbors ever. I'll make you one of my famous chocolate zucchini cakes as soon as it dies down a little here." She laughed.

In the creatively decorated "cars" room at the pediatric office, Allon screamed bloody murder as Maria undressed him. Abbie was cackling gleefully at Eula.

"Different as night and day, these two, but they like being close to each other," Maria said as she took Abbie's tiny hand and placed it over Allon's. He purred like a kitten. "It's amazing, isn't it? I think he gets mad in the car because he can't feel her."

"Well, it makes sense. They spent nine months in the womb together," Eula responded.

A light tap at the door signified the doctor's arrival. He wasted no time getting to the seriousness of the situation.

"See this growth chart. Abbie is going on a nice curve, but Allon is not. In fact, his is sloping downward. This shows failure to thrive. It can be serious and even fatal if we do not get a handle on it now. I want you to increase his feedings. Double the amount you give him and add this mixture. It is dense with protein and nutrients," the doctor ordered. "I'll see you back in two months. If he's not improving, we may need to initiate a feeding tube." He stood to leave.

"But wait. He throws up the four ounces I give him now. How can I get him to eat more?" Maria panicked.

"Mrs. Frigmann, be patient. Feed him two ounces every hour until he does hold it down. Do whatever you need to. Normally with drug-addicted babies, especially twins, one thrives above the other, and one tends to be sickly and a runt. If he were a pig, the mother and other piglets would root him out, and he would starve to death. Thankfully, that is not the case, but I can assure you, you only want to place a feeding tube if it's absolutely necessary. Give my regards to your husband." He turned and walked out.

"Well, he has the bedside manner of a snake," Eula puffed.

"Oh, Mom, I wish Brian were home. He'd know exactly what to do. I feel like if Allon bonded with me more, he would eat more. I ran out of the flower syrup Brian made me two days ago. He was doing better until then. I need to try harder, but there are many distractions. You and Dad being here will help. Thank you." Maria buried her head into her mom's shoulder.

"Maybe you should try something different. He is old enough to have almond milk and cereal. Put a small amount in a bowl and feed him little bites. See what happens. Do it while we are here," her mom encouraged.

The miombo trees swayed with the same limber vitality of the tall palms in Arizona. The group stopped to eat fruits and honey for strength. Brian's eye grew wide as he watched the thin, dark-skinned man scale his way up the branches. The bees buzzing around the man's head did not faze him in his endeavor to collect more honey from the hive. Ever so gently, he reached into the hive collecting some of the comb and filling his leather pouch with the thick, amber gooeyness. Never once did he swat at them or make a sudden move. Everything was done intentionally, instinctively. These men learned from childhood how to use the bounty of the woodlands, ocean, and savannah to survive. The fish they caught and cooked the night before would be their meal for several days of the journey. The fish were wrapped carefully in the miombo leaves and vanilla bark to cover the scent. They did not want any predators attracted to its smell.

The stories these men told of their childhood adventures were more than amazing; they were extremely family-oriented. Angel begged for a tale or two every time they stopped to rest or sleep. Unlike the serious Neatorama tribe, these men could defend with honor but laugh with intensity, their bright teeth shining through their broad smiles.

As they walked through the clearing from the forest to the savannah that lay before them, Brian began to sing, "Over the mountains and through the woods, to grandmother's house we go."

Angel chimed in, her voice radiant with song. As she brushed the top of the thick leaves with her hand, she screamed in pain, lurching it away. Brian immediately yanked her from his shoulders. The men surrounded them. She began to quiver and cry. The swelling in her right hand was instant.

"What is it?" Brian demanded.

One of the men grabbed her hand and took a knife to cut it.

"Wait! Stop!" Brian yelled.

"No, we have to do this now!" he pushed Brian away. The other men held him and fear of infection plagued his mind.

Angel's eyes flowed with tears.

"Trust me little one." One of the men held her as he sliced through the needlepoint mark and sucked the poison out, spitting it on the ground. He sent one of the men to look for a certain plant to protect from infection. They packed the wound and wrapped it with cloth torn from the cleanest garment they could find.

"You're very brave. You may feel hot, a little sick at your tummy, and tired; the cut is deep, but it will heal. You'll be okay. Drink." He held water to her mouth and then gently embraced her.

The men let their guard down, and Brian tore away from them and ran to his daughter.

Rojomen's brother put his hand up. "She's okay, my friend. The jungle spider is extremely poisonous; it would make an adult very sick, but it would mean death for a child, if the poison spread through the bloodstream. I'm sorry." He handed Angel to him.

Chapter Fifteen
ANYTHING IS POSSIBLE

Barbie reveled in the hours spent by the pool working on her mother's story. The journals she inherited left a legacy of healing, which kept giving her publishing material. The warm Arizona sun shone, dazzling off the crystal water of the pool. Unfortunately, her peaceful morning was invaded by children, which she normally loved.

"No getting distracted today. I have a deadline," she murmured, but decided to watch the scenario unfold.

The two-year-old cried as his mom pulled him from the water kicking and screaming with his water floaties bobbing in the air. She consoled, "Honey, we've got to eat a snack, or your belly will hurt. Stop throwing a fit, and we'll come back in shortly."

The two older children were already seated under the metal umbrella waiting for their grandfather to unpack the food. "Come on, Papa, we're hungry," the older boy fussed.

"You're always hungry." He laughed as he handed them both a peanut butter and jelly sandwich. The towhead boy calmed down and climbed into his Papa's lap. The old man gently wiped his eyes. "Here, big boy. Eat up."

They ate quickly and started to jump back in, but he stopped them. "Not yet. Drink some water and rest a few minutes. I'll tell you a story," he said.

"Oh, Papa," the little girl murmured.

"Yeah!" yelled the two-year-old, clapping his hands.

Even though the older children squirmed in their metal chairs, they were intently glued on their grandfather's exuberant and bright eyes. His stories came alive as he exaggerated the adventures of hunting in the safaris of Africa. He growled like a tiger, hissed like a snake, and used his voice and hands to make the thunderous noise of a summer storm. The children were mesmerized until the youngest jumped down and started hollering, "Pool! Pool!"

"Okay, good job. We'll finish our story time later." He let them go.

Barbie's phone rang. "Hello. Oh, hi honey. Yes, I'm at the pool working. No, you're not bothering me. Maria called you? She does. Okay. I'll meet you back at the apartment."

Brian wrapped his arms around his little girl. She snuggled deeply into his chest.

"It's okay, Daddy. I'm alright," Angel consoled him.

"I know, honey. God has made you strong. Rest now," Brian encouraged.

As he held her, he thought of how much these native African people had transformed their lives, from the moment Rojomen placed Angel in their arms and even now. "Thank you, Lord," he whispered as he rocked her back and forth. "What would life be like without them now that Angel would be theirs and her life was no longer threatened?" Brian contemplated.

It had been a long day. The men decided to make camp and give Angel time to rest. The stars twinkled brightly in the midnight sky. Brian fell asleep holding his pint-size princess. She ran a slight fever in the night but it broke before the sun shone the next morning.

"Doctor, we must go." Someone pressed lightly on Brian's shoulder. "The convoy will not wait."

"Yes, okay." He gently shook Angel, but she did not want to waken.

"Mommy. Mommy," she cried.

"It's okay, honey. We'll see Mommy soon, but we must go," Brian consoled. Strong arms reached to take her, but she clung to Brian.

"I have her. Help me up, please," he pleaded.

The man grabbed Brian's free hand and pulled him to his feet, steadying him and the child in his arms.

"Fever?" the man asked with stern brow.

"Yes, it broke in the night.

"Good!" he smiled.

The entourage fell in ranks with Brian carrying Angel in the middle. The child slept for hours, and he grew concerned. Her breathing and heartbeat seemed normal. The best thing would be to get her to the city. Then he could take her in and get a thorough exam. The men's pace quickened, and Brian could barely keep up. Their gentle, strong friend patted Brian on the shoulder and took Angel from his numb arms.

"It'll be okay," he said. "We must hurry. We're running out of time, but we're almost there."

Brian's legs burned with brute intensity as they began a run through the wide-open range. The sun beat down on their brows and sweat dripped in and stung his eyes. Wiping with his hand or arm only made it worse. One of the men in the lead starting hollering and waving his arms violently. The convoy was moving.

"No, Lord, please," Brian begged. "We're too close not to make it."

Then like a gazelle the tall, thin man began a sprint, none like Brian had ever seen.

The brown, green and tan jeeps haltered.

"Thank God!" he yelled.

Angel woke up. "Daddy!"

Brian took her from the man and swung her into the air. "Look, we're here. We'll be home soon."

The men each knelt down and gave Angel a hug. Brian thought he could see tears in their eyes. He grabbed the brother who had carried his child and embraced him. "Thank you. Thank all of you."

The man who suffered shock and injury from the stampede refused Brian's offer to take him to the hospital. His strength seemed to miraculously come back, but Brian wanted him to see a doctor in the city. Their journey through the continent of Africa shaped their love for the people of the woodland forever. They would never forget. He was able to get some supplies in the city and gave Angel a quick exam before their plane took off.

This land of magical mystery and miracles would soon be behind them. Brian did not have time to find a phone and call Maria. It would have to wait until they got stateside. On the plane Angel drew pictures of the animals they had seen: delightful giraffes with long necks and vibrant orange color, large grey elephants, long green snakes, and a stately lion roaring. She drew stick people to represent the men, one with a broad smile and big arms and Brian holding her hand. On the other page she colored a house with Maria, Joshua, and the twins.

"What are those spots?" Brian asked.

"Mommy's tears. She misses us!" she exclaimed.

"She certainly does." Brian patted her hand. He began to think of all the excitement there would be when they arrived home. Of course, there would be a lot of explaining and rest for Maria. He did not know if he would even have a job. This trip could change their lives forever, in more ways than Brian could even begin to understand.

Maria paced back and forth in the corridor of the courthouse.

"Sweetie, come sit down," her mom called.

She sat beside Eula. "Mom, what am I going to tell the judge?" I've not heard from Brian in weeks. I don't even know if they're okay, or when he'll be back? I could lose them all." Maria sobbed.

"Breathe. God knows, and he didn't bring you this far to drop you off. Mindfulness. Remember, you can't entertain those other thoughts. He'll give you the words to tell the judge. He's your defender. The twins are doing wonderful, well, comparatively speaking. You're doing an amazing job. Besides, this isn't a hearing. Consider it more of a checkup," Eula consoled.

"Mrs. Frigmann, the judge will see you now," the assistant stated.

Maria wheeled the double-stroller down the long hall to the magistrate's office. The massive redwood pillars loomed above her, and her shaking legs nearly buckled. She breathed deeply and told herself, "Get it together, girl. Who are you trusting, yourself or Jesus? If you can take care of twins and a toddler, you got this!" The pep talk worked, and she held her body with confidence as the officer opened the door for Maria.

"Hello, Maria, come in." The judge stood, walked around her desk, and extended her hand. "My, have they grown since I saw you last."

"Yes, they have. Thank you," Maria responded.

"Have a seat. You look a little flushed. Is everything okay?" she asked.

"Oh, yes. Not much sleep these days." Maria pointed to the twins and laughed nervously.

Well, don't worry. This is not a hearing. I just wanted to see how things are going. The papers from Beatrice came across my desk to relinquish Joshua's custody to you and your husband. Speaking of Brian, where is he?" the judge inquired.

"He's working in a remote region of Africa. I'm hoping to hear from him soon. My parents have been helping with the children," Maria responded.

"Very well. When he returns I'll need to meet with both of you to finalize the adoption papers for Joshua. I'm very proud of the way you've handled the whole situation with the grandparents. Losing a child, adult or not, is devastating and a detrimental blow to any parent."

Abbie started to cry. Maria unbuckled her and quickly scooped her up into her arms, rubbing the side of her head, and consoling her. Her brother slept right through the commotion.

The judge smiled. Maria's phone rang, "I'm sorry." She reached to shut it off but realized it was Brian's ring tone. "Judge, pardon me, I must get this call. It's Brian." Maria started to step out but remembered Allon.

The judge nodded. "It's okay. I have him."

"Hello. Honey, where are you?" Maria whispered.

"It's good to hear your voice too," Brian remarked.

"Mommy!" Angel declared jubilantly.

Maria's eyes welled with tears as Angel rattled off excitedly about her new baby brother and other family.

"That's wonderful, darling. I can't wait to see you. I love you. We'll talk all about it when you get home. I need to talk to Daddy now," Maria replied as she braced herself against the wall.

"I'll explain everything when we get home. We're boarding. Gotta go. Love you to the moon and back," Brian said as he hung up the phone.

"Where are you?" Her words trailed off into oblivion as she heard the space go numb. "They're coming home; that's all that matters. Did you hear that, Abbie? Your daddy and sissy are coming home?"

She took a deep breath to pull herself together and quietly entered the room again. She looked up to see the judge holding Allon.

"They are adorable and looking heathier and happier every time I see you. Good news?" The judge asked.

"Yes, they are on their way home." Maria beamed, her eyes now radiant with excitement.

"I'm going to sign the papers for Joshua as soon as Brian returns. We'll continue the legal process for the twins' adoption, so you have good news too," the judge replied.

Maria stood to shake her hand but asked if she could hug her instead.

"Of course." She gave her a gentle side hug because she still held the baby.

"Thank you. I can't tell you how happy I am," Maria said gratefully.

The Judge handed Allon to Maria. She buckled both the babies in the stroller and walked to the door. Maria practically ran to her mom and collapsed in her arms crying.

"What's wrong?" her mom demanded.

"Nothing, everything is perfect. We're adopting Joshua and the twins. Brian and Angel are on their way home. We'll be a family again!" she exclaimed.

"Hallelujah! Praise the Lord!" Eula shouted. "When will they be here?"

"I don't know. He didn't have much time. All I know is they are on a plane headed to us from somewhere," Maria responded.

"Maybe we should go to your house, pack everyone up, and head to ours; you'll be in Phoenix when they arrive," Eula stated.

"Sounds good. Thanks, Mom. You mean the world to me." Maria hugged her.

Abbie threw her sippy cup on the ground. Allon started laughing.

"It's a game now." Maria scooped it up and put it in her purse.

"Oh, your dad called and said Joshua is running a slight fever. I'm sure it's nothing to worry about, probably getting his two-year molars in," Eula informed.

"Yeah, pray. I'm going to the lounge to feed them. Want to help, and then we can head home?" Maria asked.

Maria gave Joshua a little Hyland's teething medicine, filled his brown doggie back pack, made him a sippy cup, and hugged her parents' bye. "I'll see y'all in a few hours. I might try to nap a few minutes while they are sleeping before I head down. My adrenaline is kicking in. Sleeping may be out of the question; if so, I'll get a chai and be on my way. May God put angels in the front, to the back and all sides, take you through dangers, seen and unseen, and bring you safely home, in Jesus' name. There, now you're set. Need anything else?" Maria asked.

"No, I think we're good to go." Eula hugged her. "See you soon."

Maria tried to sleep, but it was impossible. She packed the twins' needs in their diaper bags and her items in the only suitcase left in the house, loaded all of it and the babies in the car, and got on the road.

Barbie called on the way down, "Do you still need Ken to check Allon out? We're on our way to Sedona. We thought we could come by your way first?"

"No, but where are you now?" Maria questioned.

"We're about an hour from Camp Verde. Why?" Barbie asked.

"Meet me at Starbucks at the Camp Verde exit. I need to talk to you. I don't want to tell you on the phone," Maria responded.

"Do you care if we stop in CV to meet Maria? It sounds important." Barbie asked Ken and then turned her voice back to Maria. "He said that would be fine."

"Awesome! See you there." Maria hung up and switched on the radio. "Thank you, Lord. It will be refreshing to see my best friend."

The song "Good, Good Father" played on the radio and for a minute Maria lost herself in the moment, praising the Lord for His manifold blessings and sang with all her might. Unfortunately, this woke both twins, and they cried mercilessly all the way down the mountain. She made it to a rest area before she could pull over. There she sat in the middle of the two car seats and fed them, propping Allon up more to keep him from spitting up. Even though it was time-consuming, the instructions the pediatrician had given was working. Maria mixed it in almond milk with a little cereal, like her mom suggested. It was producing results as he slowly gained weight. Abbie was twice the size of Allon as she guzzled down everything she could get her mouth on and ate the baby food too.

Maria burped each baby and then sang to them. "We must get back on the road, my darlings," she said as she buckled them in. "Daddy is coming home." Allon smiled and Abbie cackled as Maria made a funny face toward them. She snapped a picture and sent it to Brian's cell phone. "These two can't wait until you get home; neither can I. Expect to get a lot of love and attention."

Barbie and Ken were sitting in a corner making goo-goo eyes at each other when Maria arrived. When they realized she was there, they quickly went to the vehicle to help her. There was a cool breeze blowing, and she rolled the windows down. "Do you mind if we talk right here? They're sleeping, and I don't want to wake them." Maria asked.

She got out of the car and walked around the door to give them a hug.

"What's up?" Barbie asked.

"Hey, why don't I sit in the car with the twins and you two go over there and talk?" Ken offered.

"A gentleman and a babysitter, wow! You can't ask for more than that." Maria laughed.

"Thanks, hon." Barbie kissed him.

Maria shared all about what was happening with the children and about Brian coming home with Angel. She told her things she had not been able to share in seven years. They held each other and cried; they rejoiced together.

"I know you are getting married and starting your own family, but you'll always be a part of mine. I hope we'll remain close. Ken seems real nice, and he's good to you, right?" Maria questioned.

"Yes, better than any man ever has been. The wedding will be soon, maybe even in Sedona or California; I'm torn. You'll be the first to know. It will be immediate family only, and your family is mine. Pastor Stroke will officiate. I love you sister," Barbie shared.

"Thank you. I'm happy for you. I'll let you know as soon as Brian arrives home. After he's rested, we will have a party. Pray for us. We'll have some big decisions to make, but our family is complete just like the picture on Angel's wall. God answered every prayer. I love you too," Maria responded.

Chapter Sixteen
LOVE FULFILLED

"The captain has ordered everyone to return to their seats and keep their seat belts tightly fastened, please," the airline flight attendant ordered.

"Ma'am, what's happening?" Brian inquired.

She ignored him and headed to the back. The captain's jovial voice rang loud and clear through the overhead speaker. "Please, be seated. We'll be having unusually turbulent weather ahead. I'm trying to get us above the storm, but we may hit the tail end of the wind currents. Hope everyone was listening carefully when instructions were given earlier. We're about there. Hold on tight cowboys, this steer is about to try and bump us." He said imitating a Texas drawl. He laughed easing everyone's tension. "It'll be okay, folks. I'll let you know when it is safe to move about."

In minutes the plane started swaying back and forth, bobbing up and down, then abruptly took a brief nose dive. Oxygen masks flew from their overhead compartments. People started screaming. Brian held Angel's hand, gently placed her oxygen mask on and prayed. He turned her face toward him.

"Jesus did not bring us this far to let us crash. It will be okay," he assured her.

A lady close to the front row began to holler, "Help! Help! I think he is having a heart attack!"

"Stay here. I'll be right back," Brian told Angel.

He looked at the stewardess in disbelief as she sat frozen in her chair. "Ma'am, where is your first aid kit? I'm a doctor." The turbulence threw the plane sideways, and Brian crashed hard into the emergency exit door, fell onto a lady's foot, and hit his head. "Are you okay?" she yelled.

He stumbled as he got up, but managed to say, "Yes."

"You're bleeding." She handed him a napkin. "Dr. Frigmann? Is it really you?"

"Yes, but I need to go help the gentleman in the front row. Are you okay?" he said, not recognizing her.

"I'm fine. I can help. I'm a nurse," she responded.

They held the sides of the chairs and methodically made their way down the aisle. Brian glanced back at Angel to make sure she was okay. An elderly lady scooted over next to her and held her hand. Brian checked the man's pulse. The man was unresponsive.

"Help me pull him to the floor. Carefully now," Brian said as he unbuckled him. "Look for a nitro tab in the emergency kit. I'll start CPR. Ask the flight attendant if there is a defibrillator on board, please."

The lady next to the man's seat sobbed. "Help him, please."

"Are you his wife? Has he had any heart issues in the past? Ma'am, I need your help, please," Brian insisted.

"Yes, he had a heart attack about fifteen years ago. He was only fifty-one at the time. He's had no problems since then. They put one stint in due to the blockage," she replied. "He worries all the time. I try to tell him not too, but he won't listen. He says it's his job to worry."

The plane pulled violently up and sent Brian flying face forward into the aisle. "Come on, guy; get this under control. Jesus, we need your help." He shouted, shaking himself and standing to his feet in battle mode, "Devil, get your grimy hands off this plane in Jesus' name!" He walked over and placed his hands on the man's chest. "I speak life to you in Jesus' name." Then he listened to his heart again.

"Ma'am, do I have your permission to use this machine to try to get his heart beating again? After I do so, I'll start an IV, if I have your permission," he pleaded.

"Yes! Please!" the wife begged.

The nurse helped Brian place the leads on, set the defibrillator, and he placed the paddles to the man's chest. They shocked him twice. The small portable monitor started alarming, beep, beep, beep, beep.

"Okay, his heart is extremely weak. We need to place this IV. I need to talk to the captain. Can you handle it?" he asked.

The girl confidently responded, "Yes, sir, I can."

Brian waved at Angel and gave her a thumbs up. He went to the head flight attendant. "I need to talk to the captain immediately. We've a critical situation."

"It won't be possible. We've strict orders during emergency settings not to open the cabin door. However, you could talk to him on the phone by the door," she pertly replied.

"I wouldn't expect anything less." Brian said as he followed her. He picked up the receiver and spoke to the captain, "Sir, we've a dire circumstance here. How soon will we be out of this weather? Okay, we need to land at the nearest airport. A man on board suffered a severe heart attack. His heart is responding but weak. He needs to be airlifted to a hospital asap. Thank you. I'll try to keep the others calm." Brian hung up the phone and turned to the attendant, "Put me on the passenger phone. Now, please. I've orders from the captain. 'Ladies and gentlemen, take a deep breath and hold for ten seconds. Listen, we are going to be okay. I'm Dr. Frigmann. The captain said we are three-quarters of the way through the worst part of the storm. Bear with him and try not to panic. He's doing his best to get us to safety. He needs everyone's cooperation. Stay seated. Thank you,'" Brian announced.

"Stephanie, I recognize you now. I treated you when you were sixteen. Wow, look at you now. Glad to see you are doing well. Wish it were under different circumstances. Did you get the IV in?" he said.

"No, every time I try, the plane shifts, and I'm not sure his veins are very good. Look at this." She pointed to a shriveled-looking area.

"He's dehydrated. Let me try," he said.

"Great job, Dr. Brian," she applauded.

"Okay, now you buckle back up. I'll stay here next to him. Thank you," He commanded.

"Is he going to be okay?" the wife asked Stephanie.

"We hope so. The captain will get us to the nearest airport, and an emergency crew will be waiting there for us," she consoled.

Brian faced Angel as he held the man's head in his lap and tried to stabilize his body. Her little head strained to see above the back of the chairs, but she put her nose through the seats to get an eye on him, and he winked at her. He had a massive headache and his hip hurt, but the man was alive; everything else seemed trivial at the moment.

Maria waited anxiously by the phone at her parent's home. The news had announced Brian and Angel's plane was delayed due to unexpected turbulence and an emergency landing. "I can't believe this," she fussed. "They are in Texas. We could drive and get them by the time they will be back in the air. Why doesn't he call?" She asked.

"He is probably helping the passengers. He is a doctor. You know his compassionate heart. Calm down. He'll call soon," Eula quipped.

"You're right. I'm sorry. Dad, will you get Joshua? He is teething and needs some gel. Please and thank you," she said as her father stood to do as she asked.

Eula selected a movie on Netflix. "Bring your tea and come sit down. You know a watched phone never rings."

"Mom, doesn't it go, 'a watched pot never boils?'" Maria remarked.

"Maybe, but this applies for now." She patted the seat next to her. "Look, we'll watch one of our all-time favorites, *Anne of Green Gables*. We used to watch it once or twice a year when you were a girl. Your dad would always take off when we put it in. Did you know he'll now watch the entire series with me? They've a kid's version now. Maybe I'll get it for Angel for Christmas or her birthday," Eula commented.

They made it through the first movie and were about to watch the second when Maria jumped up to make popcorn. "You know the twins will be up any minute. We'll need to put this on pause. It did relax me."

"Maria, your cell phone is ringing. I'll get it," Eula bellowed. "Hello, yes, she is. Glad to hear your voice. Hi, my sweet Angel. Mema misses you too. We'll see you soon."

Maria reached her hand out for the phone. "Mom, come on," she voiced.

Eula handed her the phone. "They are safe. Hallelujah! I'll go fix the bottles."

"Oh, honey. I'm glad you called. I was worried sick. The news never gives enough information. Oh no, is he okay? You'll be home in the morning. Hallelujah! We'll see you then. I love you both to the moon and back." Maria collapsed on the couch. "Thank you, Lord!"

"They are good. Exhausted maybe, but good," Eula responded. "What time do we pick them up?" she asked, handing Maria a bottle and Allon. "Don't look at me like that. He won't eat for anybody but you. I'll get Abbie."

Aaron walked in with Joshua. "He won't go back to sleep. He keeps asking for you."

"It's okay. Brian called. Daddy is coming home, Joshua." She encouraged her two-and-a-half-year-old son. He came over and climbed up beside her, burying his head in her side and clinging to his blankie. "Their plane lands at 11:00 a.m. They'll be famished, so we'll all go for a late breakfast. Brian may want to go straight home. You know how he is. It'll be his decision. I'm overwhelmed at God's goodness and thankful they're coming home." Now to get everyone fed and in bed, Maria whispered.

The doctor at the memorial hospital told Brian he wanted him to stay for twenty-four observation due to being thrown around the aircraft and the cut on his head, but he said no. He politely informed the emergency room staff he would be going to a hotel for the night and home the next morning. Everyone applauded his acts of bravery and courage in helping the man. Brian saved his life. He and Stephanie were able to talk for a few minutes on their commute to the hospital. She had overcome her depression, made amends with her parents, and finished her nursing degree. Her next goal was to enter medical school. She shared with him how his kindness had saved her life and given her new reason to live; accepting Jesus love and forgiveness was the best thing she had ever done. It freed her like nothing ever had. She also used her pain to minister to young women who had been raped, abused, and who had received abortions, letting them know there is healing, forgiveness, and hope through sharing a song called, "Jesus Rocking Chair." He was elated and agreed to keep in touch.

As Brian tucked Angel in bed, he thought about the men who sacrificed to get them home. They would journey the same way home they came. He wondered if they were safe and prayed for them. He thanked God for using him to save the man on the plane. The events that happened on the plane solidified his call to be a doctor, dispelling the discouraging political tides threatening to sweep his gifting away. The next step was up to God; he would go wherever God called him, and he had a feeling it would be far away from where they lived now.

At 4:00 a.m. the buzzer on the hotel alarm blared, waking the dead. 'What an annoying sound," Brian said as he reached over and turned it off. "Oh, my goodness." He yawned and headed for the shower. Before he could turn the water on, his phone rang.

"Good morning, early bird," Maria whispered.

"Wow! You're up early. Did one of the kids wake you?" Brian teased.

"No, I knew you'd be up early, and this is the only quiet time we'll have for a while. I wanted to hear your voice in the stillness of the night, without the little ones interrupting. The twins are almost sleeping through the night. We've had some tough challenges while you were away; I've a lot to tell you. What happened with Angel?" she asked.

"Honey, she is ours. The tribe set her free. I'll explain why later, but it's like Rojomen said, 'Trust me.' He kept saying it over and over again, but it was hard. I didn't want to lose her. God worked it all out for good. No matter what happens with the other children, they'll always be ours deep inside. We'll be all right. God is good all the time," he replied.

"All the time, God is good. Do you want to stay at Mom and Dad's for the weekend? They can help us with the kids, and we can have time to talk. If we go home, we'll get into the parent and work mode. There'll be no time. Please." She paused. "I've good news for you too. It'll wait until you get home. I miss you. I've longed for your arms wrapped around me. My biggest fear was you would never come home. I was scared too," Maria responded.

"Sounds good. I don't care where we are, as long as I'm with you. Have you received any mail from the hospital? My boss left me an ugly message on my phone. I wasn't able to get it until yesterday.

I may not have a job. I know God's prepared something special for us to do. We've my 401K and our savings to fall back on, if they let me go. We'll be okay. I can't wait to see you, my love. I need to hop in the shower and then get Angel up. I love you to the moon and back, my sweet darling," Brian flirted.

"I love you too. You mean more to me than all the flowers covering this planet. See you tomorrow, my lover," Maria said in a sultry tone.

They hung up the phone, and she went into welcome home mode. She quietly dug out her mom's craft markers and poster board from the den closet. She printed a copy of the vision picture hanging in Angel's bedroom and elegantly wrote the meaning of each child's name by their representative in the portrait.

Isaiah – The Lord is generous.

Angel – Messenger

Joshua Aaron – Jehovah saves and is generous.

Abbie – My Father rejoices.

Allon -Strong as an oak

In large, bold letters, she wrote, Welcome Home, Daddy. We love you!

Welcome Home, Sissy. We love you too!

She scribbled each of the children's names as if they signed it themselves. At the bottom she copied the verse, "Children are a heritage from the Lord!"

Next, she organized their belongings and washed a load of clothes, making extra bottles for the twins and packing snacks for the older two. The coffee pot hummed its morning tune, percolating a delicious aroma of cinnamon and chocolate. Her mom combined two of her favorite flavors, making a delightful blend tantalizing even non-coffee drinkers. She knew the judge would not be in her office today, but she left a message anyway, letting her know Brian would be back in town next week if they wanted to schedule the paper signing appointment.

Maria did everything she could think of to prepare for their arrival and to make the transition home easier. She wanted to spend as much time with Brian as possible before he went back to work or started looking for another job. The idea of him losing his current employment frightened her a little because it meant, more than likely, they would be uprooting their family again. She pushed those thoughts aside and focused on them coming home. When her mom woke up, she went to the store to purchase the items to make Brian's favorite lasagna dish and one other meal option. Joshua accompanied her, and the twins stayed with her parents. They picked out balloons and flowers, singing lively songs as they made their way through Fry's.

"Hey buddy," Maria said as she tickled him. "We need to call Nanna and Papa. They'll want to know what's happening." She dialed Bea's phone, but the answering machine picked up. "Good morning. Oh, I forgot how early it is, sorry. You're probably still sleeping, but we're excited. Brian and Angel will be home today! If you want to pop over tonight for dinner at my mom's, there will be plenty. Blessings. Love you." "Say, 'Love you,'" she encouraged Joshua, and he did. "He stretched out his arms wide that time. See you later," Maria said.

"I'm glad your nanna and I are friends," she said as she hugged him.

"Me too." He squirmed.

"Angel, wake up honey. We need to get you dressed." Brian called his sleeping child. "We're going home today. You get to see Mommy, your brothers and sisters, and Mema and Papa," he gently persisted.

She yawned and rolled over to look him in his deep blue eyes. "Daddy, your eyes are pretty."

"Thank you. You're lovely, my dear. Now, would you like to wear your princess outfit today, the one Rojomen gave you?" Brian asked.

"Oh yes!" She jumped up and engulfed him with her arms. "Thank you."

Brian wanted to honor the sacrifices the chief, Rojomen, and their family made. He dressed her exactly like the nanny taught him, with the ornamental beads and tiara. She looked like a princess from the fairytale books they read to her, except she looked more realistic and exquisite. There was no question about it, the teen years would be a challenge with this doll, boys chasing her down. He laughed out loud. "We'll cross that bridge when we get there. God help us all."

"What bridge, Daddy?" Angel asked as she twirled around in her native dress.

"I'll explain when you get a little older. Go brush your teeth. We'll eat downstairs before we travel to the airport. Make sure we pray. The weather looks good all the way. We've nothing to fear." He made a point to dispel her fears before they started.

The pilot stopped Brian as he boarded the plane. "We heard of what happened on your last flight. We've bumped you and your daughter up to first class. It's our way of saying thank you. Order anything you want. It's on me."

"Thank you, very kind of you," he responded.

The flight attendant brought Angel a coloring book and crayons. "We heard you like almond milk. Here you go." She handed Angel a kids' carton of chocolate almond milk. "You're a brave one and look how pretty you are."

"Thank you. Yummy!" Angel licked her lips.

"Yes, thank you. What a special treat." He turned to the lady. "May I have a glass of red wine, a small cup, and do you have a pack of saltines, please?" Brian asked.

"Most certainly. I'll be right back." She strode to the front of the plane.

He turned to Angel. "Let's put this stuff down for a moment." He lowered her tray table. "Do you remember how Pastor Stroke served us communion at church?"

She nodded her head yes, her dark eyes beaming.

Brian continued, "We weren't home last week, and we missed it. I think we should take communion now, re-committing our lives to Jesus and honoring him for all he has done for us on this trip. If there is anything in our hearts we need to ask forgiveness for, now is the time. I'll ask Jesus to forgive me for not trusting Him with you. We'll bow our heads and each say a silent prayer, then take the communion together. Do you have any questions?"

"Yes, I understand, except what do you mean you didn't trust Jesus?" Angel asked.

"Well, when we were in the woodlands I was afraid you would stay there with your other daddy and that I would have to let you go. But look, here you are! I'm thankful. We need to always trust Him, even when we don't think we are going to get what we want. Always," Brian explained.

"Like when you tell me no about having something I want really bad?" she said.

"Yes, you are a smart girl. Would you like to pray?" Brian grabbed her hand.

They bowed their head. "Jesus, thank you for this wonderful adventure. Help me draw it in my color sheets, angels all around us as we go home. Get us safely to Mommy. Bless all my family and the nice people on this plane. Thank you for my chocolate milk. Amen," she uttered.

"Powerful prayer. Good job!" the attendant spoke as she handed Brian the sacraments.

"Thank you!" Angel piped up.

The flight was uneventful, except for a pregnant lady getting sick and asking for help. Brian suggested the flight attendant serve her ginger ale and crackers. He smiled uneasily as a man from the back of their section made his way up and knelt beside him. He was a journalist and wanted to know why Angel was dressed in royal African attire.

He thanked him for his interest, and as Angel slept, he quietly told the man about the princess stories they told Angel since her infancy. He also explained to the man that the outfit was a gift, and he appreciated his interest, but that there was no story he wanted to tell. Brian breathed a sigh of relief when the man walked back to see his seat and thanked God his little girl slept through the entire conversation. The last thing he wanted was a nosy journalist getting ahold of her true story.

"We're about thirty minutes from landing at Phoenix International Airport; it is a lovely 92 degrees. Flight attendants, please make the cabin ready for landing," the pilot stated.

Brian took Angel to the bathroom and then secured their safety belts. The excitement was almost more than she could bear. Her little body vibrated in her chair. He held her hand and smiled at her. "You're beautiful, my Princess."

Maria and the family waited anxiously at the security gate. Aaron stayed in the parking lot waiting for their call to come around and get them. He rented a fifteen-passenger van and reserved tables at First Watch near their home. Eula held Joshua's hand, and Maria had the twins in the stroller with her homemade sign taped above them. She made Joshua a shirt reading, "I'm all yours, Daddy!"

"Please, watch your step," the pilot said as they exited the air craft.

"Thank you. Smooth landing," Brian said as they departed the plane.

As they approached the corridor to the security area, Angel jerked away from Brian and started running. She had laid eyes on her mama and there was no stopping her. Maria could not believe her eyes.

It was as if she had grown a foot. The beautifully clad child ran toward her with ferocity and tears in her eyes and a smile as wide as the river. The turquoise beads jiggled as she went, making a melody. Her tiara jiggled off her head and went crashing to the floor, stopping her in mid-sprint as she tumbled.

Angel screeched in pain and began crying. Maria thrust the stroller toward her mom and rushed to her little girl, bending down and embracing her.

"Mommy, it's broke. I'm not a princess anymore!" she wailed.

"You'll always be our princess. It's not what's on your head, what you wear or look like; it's who you are on the inside." Maria exclaimed, cuddling the child in her arms. "What's this?" She held Angel's small hand in hers.

"I got bit by a spider. The guard cut my hand and sucked the poison out, but I'm okay!" she said emphatically. "Wanna see?" Angel started to unwrap it.

Brian knelt down and gathered them to himself. "No, you leave the bandage on it. Your mom can see it later."

Before he could help them up, Joshua yelled, "Daddy! Daddy! Daddy!" and took off full throttle toward Brian.

Eula grabbed him as the security officer stood up.

Brian sprinted toward them with glee in his step, picked him up, and hugged him. "My boy! My boy!" Grateful tears spilled over; there was no stopping them.

Maria carried Angel over to them, and they did a big family group hug with the twins in the middle. He then handed Joshua to Eula. Maria sat Angel down and placed her hands on the stroller. She held Brian and kissed him. They wept.

"Dad is waiting for us. Did you read Joshua's shirt?" Maria asked.

"No, I was focused on his face. Sheer joy," Brian replied.

Eula put the boy down. He threw his arms out like instructed and danced around.

"What? He's ours?" He was speechless.

"Yes. I'll explain everything later. The judge is waiting on you to sign the papers. The papers for the twin's adoption are in process too," she responded gleefully. "I made you this poster. The children's names all match up to everything God has done and the vision he gave you." Maria could barely contain herself.

"Wow! We do have a lot to talk about." He knelt and kissed the twins on the head. "My, how they've grown. Hi, my babies! We should probably go get our luggage. Did you say your dad is waiting on us?"

"Yes. I'll text him now. It's good to have you both home," Eula pronounced.

Aaron opened the garage door, hung up the poster for Maria as she had asked, and went around to unlock the front door, letting everyone pile in from outside. He stood amazed at the colorful decorations, Maria's creativity, thinking of others' likes and going beyond expectations. "She definitely inherited those traits from her mother," he said to himself as he chuckled.

"Wait! Wait! Let me in front, please!" Maria called out. She pushed her way past each person standing at the door and handed the babies to Brian. "I've been carrying both of them for weeks. It's your turn." She giggled.

He eyed her suspiciously. "My body is jet-lagged, and what about the bump on my head?" Brian joked as he swatted her behind.

"Oh, poor baby!" Eula hollered from the back of the line. "Let's go. I've an anxious two-year-old back here."

"Almost three," Joshua said holding up four fingers.

Everyone laughed, and Eula pushed his pinkie down.

Maria opened the door and let everyone in. Purple and yellow balloons filled the air. Paper garland hung from the ceilings and a bouquet of delicate red, white, yellow, and purple flowers graced the table with a sunset cake reading, "Glad your home."

Brian laid the twins in their porta crib and twirled Maria around. "Good to be home," he said.

The poster hung in the middle of the dining room entrance in clear view and seemed magnified under the light above it. Brian read each name carefully as he looked at the children in the painting. He shouted, "God is good indeed! Thank you, Lord!"

Angel jumped up and down in jubilant celebration. Joshua mocked every move she made. The twins howled for attention among the commotion and noise. Maria picked up Abbie and handed her to Brian. She took Allon into the nursery to feed him. "I'll be back in a minute."

Eula spoke, "At breakfast you didn't finish your story about the elephants. I would like to hear the rest. Maybe we can put the kids down for a nap in a bit?"

"To be honest, Mom, I was hoping Maria and I could go out while they rested," he smirked.

"Okay, later then. I'll make her a bottle," she responded.

"Thanks for all of your help. I know Maria needed it. She's does great with all of them but it's a lot. They sure have grown." He touched Abbie's face, and she smiled. "I missed you, my pumpkin."

"Why don't you sit in my rocker and enjoy time with your babies? Joshua will play here with his trains. I'll take Angel in the kitchen and let her help me bake cookies," Eula suggested.

"Thanks, Mom." He kissed her on the cheek. "I sure could use some water, please."

"Consider it done." She handed him a bottle and burp rag. "Be careful. She guzzles. Maria is getting her use to a sippy cup too."

Brian and Maria sat outside under the cool veranda, listening and watching the peach-faced love birds and purple finches flurry around them. There was a delightful afternoon breeze, and it was unseasonably cool for the end of summer. Bergies was unusually quiet this time of day. It seemed as if the Lord cleared a pathway for their quest of a quiet date. Barbie and Ken were at the house helping Aaron and Eula entertain the children and prepare the rest of the meal for the evening. They decided to move the event outside to accommodate the guests.

"Remember the first time we met here and all the hours we spent studying in this exact spot?" Brian gazed into her emerald eyes. "Did your eyes change colors, or is it me? They never looked so beautiful. The light is dancing off them, enchanting me." He pulled her close and kissed passionately.

"Hmmm, hmmmm," was all she could manage as they locked lips and embraced. She gently pushed away. "We better stop this now. We've been an apart way too long, and well, you know…" her words trailed off.

"Okay, one more kiss. Come on. I've been craving you like you crave those chai's you get here." He tickled her ribs and pulled on her arm.

"One more!" she teased.

"Okay, tell me how you enticed Beatrice into giving us custody of Joshua. What happened?" Brian inquired as he sat back in his chair.

"I didn't. It was totally God, like from night to day. Change in an instant, well, after she tormented me a few months first. But once it happened, we became friends. She and Frederick surrendered their lives to Jesus. I'm helping her. It's a miracle! It was scary for a while with the twins. I didn't know what to do. Allon was not gaining weight, and the doctor told me it was failure to thrive and basically, if I didn't get him to eat, he could die." She rattled on and on, while Brian sat patiently listening. She paused to take a breath. "I'm sorry, I've not given you time to respond to anything. Is it too much?"

He grabbed her hand, "No, it's not. Your job is hard, and you've done a fantastic job. While I was gone I realized how much of the burden you carry in our home. I know when I work at the hospital, I'm engrossed in it. I've not had enough time with you and our children. It's going to change, probably quiet literally, maybe not by my choice. God has a plan for us. Maybe it's too soon to share this with you. I don't want to scare you. All I know is, it doesn't matter where we are, as long as I'm with you and we're obedient to the Lord, going where he sends us." He took a deep breath.

"Go ahead. I'm okay. Really. If I can handle all that's come my way over the last several months, in Jesus I can handle this. Keep in mind, God knows we can't move anywhere until the adoptions go through, and it may be a year before the twins are finalized as ours. Proceed." She tickled his arm with the tips of her fingers while gazing into his baby blues.

"I feel like Jesus is calling us somewhere far away, maybe even into a mission field. In Africa there was a tribe which had no medical care and no way to receive it. Rojomen led us through this village. I was terrified at first, mainly for Angel's health. Then God started showing me what they needed. Even though we lost some of the weakest of the people, most were saved. I shared the gospel message with them. It won't be an easy journey, and I know if you say no right now, God is speaking through you. We'll leave a heritage of caring for others with our children. They will learn to be kindhearted and to love another culture. I'm not going to lie. The country is treacherous and dangerous in many ways. Yet it's gorgeous, exhilarating, and beyond anything I can describe. I am confident God will prepare a way before us. Where he leads, he provides. There are doctors who would back a research expedition and compassion care. They would help move us into the region. It may even take a few years, but this I know, I won't go again without you. I love you," Brian explained.

"When you came to me years ago and shared the vision God gave you for our children, I thought you were crazy, and I never really saw it being fulfilled until the other day. I looked at the painting, and I was overcome by the realization of that vision, God's love fulfilled through His promise. Each of the children's names were hand-picked by Him and symbolize the reality of His goodness. Oh, Brian, I am overwhelmed." She began to weep.

He held both of her hands and prayed, "Thank you, Father God, for your goodness and providing for us a family, for answering our hearts' desire, and for showing us life is more than just about us. Your purposes are fulfilled through even our dreams. The vision you gave us is accomplished, and now we look expectantly at what you have next for us. We trust in your goodness. We ask for your wisdom and direction. Thank you for giving me a Proverbs 31 woman, she fulfills it in every way. Thank you for bringing us back together again. We love you. In Jesus' name, amen."

Maria's phone rang. "Oh my. I'm sorry, Mom. I didn't realize how late it was. Yes, please, put it in the oven. We'll be there shortly. Great! Do you want a drink? Okay. Thanks."

She could hear Barbie hollering in the background, "Yes, I want a chai."

Brian commented, "What's up? We gotta go?" He made a pouty face.

Maria leaned over and kissed him on the cheek. "Yes, it's after 6:00. Barbie wants a chai. I'm going to the restroom. I'll get it. You sit here and relax."

They all gathered around the table. Brian took a moment to look into each person's eyes. "I want each of you: Joshua, Aaron, Eula, Angel, Ken, Barbie, Frederick, Beatrice, and my sweet babies, Allie and Abbie to know how precious you are in God's sight and in ours. We are blessed and happy you could be with us tonight as we celebrate the completion of our family. I know it is bittersweet in some ways, but we cherish the heritage of each of you and of those who have gone on before us. Each one leaves a legacy in their own way. God promises to bring good out of our heartaches. He has, and he does." He looked at Joshua's grandparents with sincere compassion and gratitude. "Thank you. Adaline is proud of you. We love you. You are a part of our family. All of our children are your grandchildren, if you desire it and can handle the happy chaos." He chuckled. "Thank you, Maria, for your unconditional, persistent, and faithful love. Dad will you pray? My heart is too full right now, and I wouldn't get through it," Brian requested.

"Yes, I will. When I'm done and while you are eating, I've something I want to share." He bowed his head and all followed in sweet procession.

"Maria, this Scripture especially applies to you, even though not all of it does, because you were blessed in being able to carry Isaiah and birth him; we all watched as your heart broke and grieved at losing him. While admiring this picture, you printed and delightfully decorated for Brian with the children's names and meanings, a Scripture in Isaiah jumped into the forefront of my mind, and it seems appropriate for this time." He paused.

"No, finish your food first. Then you may have cake," Maria reprimanded Joshua. "Now, shhhh. Papa is speaking. We hear with our eyes and ears, not our mouth," she repeated.

Aaron continued, "Isaiah 54:1-5, 'Sing, barren woman, you who never bore a child; burst into song, you who were never in labor; because more are the children of the desolate woman than of her who has a husband," says the Lord.' Okay, yes, you have a husband too. But listen to this, "'Enlarge the place of your tent, stretch your tent curtains wide, do not hold back; lengthen your cords, strengthen your stakes. For you will spread out to the right and to the left; your descendants will dispossess nations and settle in their desolate cities. Do not be afraid; you will not be put to shame. Do not fear disgrace; you will not be humiliated...' Last verse, "'For your Maker is your husband-the Lord Almighty is his name-the Holy One of Israel is your Redeemer; he is called the God of all the earth.'" He read loud and strong.

Maria stood up and wrapped her arms around her dad's neck. "Thank you, Daddy. It means a lot to me. God's provided us a family. There are many blessings in the verses you read. I know there will be more children."

Brian cocked his eyebrows. "Huh? This lasagna is delicious." He was bathed in sauce. Everyone laughed.

She looked at him seriously. "You're funny. I mean spiritual children. Not only will we raise ours, by God's grace, but there are many more we'll minister to and mentor. This Scripture is confirmation of what Jesus plans on doing."

Maria walked over, took a napkin, wiped Brian's face, and kissed him gently. "I think you've something else to say before dessert."

"Cake! Cake! Cake!" Joshua and Angel started chanting. "Ice cream! Ice cream! We scream for ice cream." They laughed hysterically.

The twins started bawling simultaneously. Eula held up her hand and said, "Shhh. Let Daddy talk, and then I'll get your cake. Joshua you've one more bite." She unbuckled the twins and handed Abbie to Barbie; she placed Allon in her lap with a pacifier, rocking him back and forth.

"Welcome to our happy chaos." She winked at Beatrice.

Joshua started whimpering, but Aaron promised to help him eat his last bite. He chippered right up.

Brian stood, "May we all join hands?" he asked. "The Bible says, 'Children are a heritage of the Lord, and the fruit of the womb is his reward.' Psalms 127:3. I would say we have been richly blessed. Thank you, Lord for your abundant goodness. Even though my parents and grandparents are with you, thank you for the rich legacy of love they left me to pass down to our children. Thank you, Jesus, for our children and their families. Thank you, Father, for the healing heritage you've given us through your Son and every person here."

Is. 41:17-20, The poor and needy are seeking water when there is none; their tongues are parched with thirst. I the Lord will answer them; I, the God of Israel, will not forsake them. I will open rivers on the bare heights, and fountains in the midst of the valleys; I will make the wilderness a pool of water, and the dry land springs of water. I will plant in the wilderness the cedar, acacia, myrtle and the wild olive; I will set the cypress in the desert, the plane and the pine together. That men may see and know and consider and understand together that the hand of the Lord has done this, that the Holy One of Israel has created it. (The Everyday Life Bible – Amplified)

Alice Voyles and her husband of thirty-one years, Melvin (better known as Red), live in Arizona. They love the variety of landscape and fertile vegetation found in the dry desert oasis for those who have eyes to see it that way. Alice hopes this series has encouraged you to reach higher and gain an overcoming life through a personal, intimate relationship with the heavenly Father through Jesus Christ, his Son. You were made to be more than a conqueror, an overcomer! In her own life, Alice overcame the legacy of abuse left by men called to love her. She weathered through the storms of barrenness, not being able to conceive and bring forth children from her womb. After a difficult divorce in her early twenties, God brought her a loving husband and two beautiful daughters. She is the mom to several spiritual children (men and women she has nurtured and mentored in the Lord) who call her mom. Her heart celebrates the precious gift of her grandchildren and the close relationship she has with them.

The scripture from Isaiah in the last chapter of this book flows forth with rich living water in her life. Above all else, Alice wants you to fulfill the longings and dreams in your life, receive healing for your soul, and overcome the adversities of life, all through a relationship with Jesus Christ. She wants you to know he will never leave or forsake you! He loves you with an everlasting love! There is healing for you in His open arms!

The Bible says in Romans 10:9-10:

[9] That if you confess with your mouth the Lord Jesus and believe in your heart that God has raised him from the dead, you shall be saved.

[10] For with the heart man believeth unto righteousness; and with the mouth confession is made unto salvation. (KJV)

Prayer to Invite Jesus
to be Lord of Your Life:

"Jesus, I want to be a part of your family. You said in your word if I acknowledge and believe in my heart that you were raised from the dead, I will be saved. I accept you as Lord and Savior of my life. Thank you for forgiving me of my sin and healing the wounds of my heart. Help me forgive all who have hurt me. Thank you for your salvation. I am now saved. Jesus, you are my Lord and Savior. Thank you, Father, for forgiving, saving, and giving me eternal life with you. Amen!"

II Corinthians 5:17 says, **You** are a new creature in Jesus. Believe it. Receive it. I encourage you to read the Bible yourself. Get a version you understand and surround yourself with people who can help you grow in your relationship with Jesus. It is about a relationship, not a denomination or religion. You do need the Church (The Body of Christ).

I would love to hear how this series has impacted your life and if you have accepted Jesus as your personal Savior.

My address:

A. F. Voyles

P.O. Box 2764

Mesa, AZ 85214

My website is: alicevoylesauthor.com

a Book's Mind

Book One – *Stormy Garden*
Book Two – *Life's Oasis*
Book Three – *Eternity's Edge*
are also available for purchase on Alice's website
(alicevoylesauthor.com) or through a Book's Mind
at www.abooksmart.com.

Lookout for my future children's books
and Intimacy with God books.

If you have a book that you would like to publish,
contact Jenene Scott, Publisher, at A Book's Mind:
jenene@abooksmind.com.

www.abooksmind.com